T0130577

Deadly Sweet Tooth

Books by Kaye George

The Vintage Sweets Mysteries
Revenge is Sweet
Deadly Sweet Tooth

Coming in 2021
Into the Sweet Hereafter

Deadly Sweet Tooth

Kaye George

LYRICAL PRESS
Kensington Publishing Corp.
www.kensingtonbooks.com

LYRICAL PRESS BOOKS are published by

Kensington Publishing Corp.
119 West 40th Street
New York, NY 10018

All Kensington titles, imprints, and distributed lines are available at special quantity discounts for bulk purchases for sales promotion, premiums, fund-raising, educational, or institutional use.

Special book excerpts or customized printings can also be created to fit specific needs. For details, write or phone the office of the Kensington Sales Manager: Kensington Publishing Corp., 119 West 40th Street, New York, NY 10018. Attn. Sales Department. Phone: 1-800-221-2647.

Lyrical Press and Lyrical Press logo Reg. U.S. Pat. & TM Off.

First Electronic Edition: June 2020
ISBN-13: 978-1-5161-0541-0 (ebook)
ISBN-10: 1-5161-0541-9 (ebook)

First Print Edition: June 2020
ISBN-13: 978-1-5161-0544-1
ISBN-10: 1-5161-0544-3

Printed in the United States of America

This story is dedicated to my parents, their parents, and parents everywhere.

Acknowledgments

I must thank my son, Bret, for coming home from Thailand with dengue fever. I'm even more thankful it was just the one bout and has never recurred. (You'll see when you read the book.)

I should also thank the whole town of Fredericksburg, the wineries, the excellent restaurants, and the fine people, for being such an inspiration. I've always enjoyed my stays there and had a wonderful time. No one ever died while I was there.

Lastly, but not least, I gratefully thank my editors, Tara Gavin and Shannon Plackis, the copy editors, and the whole staff at Lyrical Press.

Chapter 1

Tally Holt had been hoping he wouldn't show up today.

While Tally was talking, pacing the floor as she heard the news she didn't want to hear, Yolanda burst into Tally's office from the kitchen of Tally's shop.

"Who was that on the phone?" asked Yolanda Bella, Tally's best friend.

Tally's friend owned Bella's Baskets, the gift basket business that was located next door to Tally's vintage sweet shop on Main Street in Fredericksburg, Texas.

Yolanda flounced into the office guest chair, her bright orange and yellow skirt billowing as she sat. *Flamboyant* was the only word for the way Yolanda dressed, in bright colors that always seemed to swish around her when she moved. They looked good with her dark coloring—wild dark brown curls and flashing eyes that were so dark, they were almost black. Tally was quite a contrast with her usual jeans and T-shirt, but, as they say, opposites attract. The two, now in their mid-thirties, were best friends going back to their school days.

"It was my brother, Cole," Tally said, stuffing her phone into her pocket.

Yolanda frowned. There was no love lost between those two. "Is he coming early?"

Tally nodded, slumping into her desk chair. "I'm afraid so. I guess it's good he wants to help, but we don't need him. He was supposed to come late Friday, and now thinks he'll get here earlier." She took a deep breath, inhaling the delicious scents of her shop, chocolate and caramel dominating today. The lingering warm fragrance had a calming effect and her shoulders lost some of their tension.

"I thought he was tied up until Friday night. Isn't he doing a big installation in Albuquerque?"

"He was. He finished early." Tally neatened the thick stack of job applications that included those she had been dealing with for the last three hours. "I think what he really wants to do is to see Dorella."

"That's good. That'll keep him out of our hair."

"You mean, keep him out of *your* hair, don't you?" Yolanda, Tally knew, would prefer for Cole to stay in Albuquerque forever. They didn't have a good history. Tally loved her brother, she just wasn't ready for him to come quite yet. There was so much to deal with.

"Hey," Yolanda said, "was the woman I saw leaving just now applying to help cater? Have y'all had a good turnout with applications?"

That was a problem. "Yes and no. I mean, I've had lots of people apply for the job, but there aren't very many I'd consider hiring to help with the reception."

Tally shuffled the job applications, pulling out the ones she'd flagged with sticky notes. They were for promising interviewees, the ones who hadn't interrupted the session for a cell phone call, hadn't texted the whole time, hadn't worn rumpled (or, in one case, dirty) clothing. The chosen few had sat up straight and paid attention to her and thoughtfully answered her questions. The number of those applicants was discouragingly small.

The reception was coming up soon, in three days. Tally wanted it to be perfect, since it was such a special occasion. Hiring people was not her favorite part of being a small-business owner. But it was necessary. The job she was interviewing people for today was a bit different. She had decided that the two or three she picked to do the reception would be considered later for a position at Tally's Olde Tyme Sweets, her vintage candy shop. Depending on how they worked out at the reception.

"How many did you talk to today?" Yolanda asked.

"Six. That's all I had time for."

"The one I saw didn't look half bad."

"I'll admit she was one of the better ones. I wish I had time to interview a whole lot more, but I have a shop to run."

"It'll be much better when you get some help in here. You're doing everything yourself."

Yolanda had an assistant, a young man named Raul, but Tally was running her place all by herself lately, having had a run of bad luck with assistants. It was mid-August and the high tourist season was in full swing. Tally needed more help to order supplies, make her candies and sweets, sell them, and do all the cleaning and neatening that needed to be constantly attended to.

"I have to get out of my office," Tally said. "I've been cooped up here for three hours." She had closed an hour early, at six, to do the interviews.

"Are y'all hungry? Let's go out and get a late supper." Yolanda jumped up. "How about that new place? Do you remember the name?"

"You mean Burger Kitchen?"

"Yes, that's it. Raul has eaten there and I think Kevin has, too."

"Perfect. Let's do it." Tally took one more look at the applications, stuck three of them into her purse, and followed Yolanda. After she locked the back door from the inside, they went out through the shop at the front, Tally pausing a moment to enjoy looking over the salesroom she had worked so hard on, had poured her heart and her money into.

Muted pinks and lilacs swirled across the walls, accented with chocolate brown shelving, and lit with cute lights whose shades looked like mason jars. The glass display cases gleamed. They'd better, Tally thought, since she had polished them after closing, as she did every night.

She and Yolanda walked across the rustic, wide-plank flooring to the front door and left, accompanied by the soft chimes activated by opening the door.

"Oh gosh, Nigel! I forgot about him," Tally said when they were on the sidewalk outside. "He'll be rummaging through the cupboards and opening cereal boxes if I don't get home and feed him. I'll meet you there."

"Do you mind if Kevin joins us?" Yolanda asked.

Tally smiled. She didn't mind at all. "Of course not."

In fact, she was delighted that a relationship was developing between Yolanda and Kevin Miller. He was the proprietor of Bear Mountain Vineyards, the wine shop on the other side of Bella's Baskets. Seeing as both Tally and Yolanda were business owners, the two women were able to collaborate sometimes, using Tally's treats to help fill Yolanda's gift baskets. Despite spending so much time together, it was only a week or so ago that Tally realized something was happening between Kevin and Yolanda. Kevin was older than Yolanda, maybe by ten years or so, but they hit it off well.

It was a quarter past nine, well after sunset. Even though the sun had set, the hot air rippled with excited shoppers and locals on their way to get something to eat or drink, or to see some of the entertainment offerings in the quaint, Texas tourist town. The area around Fredericksburg was studded with many wineries and the German town boasted quite a few tasting rooms.

"See you in about twenty minutes." Tally turned to go the other direction to her rental house, which was only four blocks away.

"We'll save you a seat."

* * * *

When Tally opened the front door to her small, neat ranch house, she wasn't met with the noisy greeting that had become usual over the last few weeks that Nigel had lived with her.

He's mad, she thought. That won't be good. She threw her purse onto the couch, peering around the living room for him.

"Here, Nigel," she crooned. "Come get your dinner." It wasn't until she poured the kibble into his bowl that he appeared, drawn by the clatter. The huge, black and white Maine coon cat gave a disgusted glance in her direction, then went straight to his task, extracting morsels and setting them gently on the mat so he could eat them. Tally had finally gotten a couple of mats for his dining pleasure so she could toss them into the washing machine when they got full of kibble crumbs. Before the mats, she had to scrub the floor around his food and water bowls every other day.

He was not about to do anything so common as to eat from his own food bowl.

She smiled at the haughty cat. Her life had been simpler but, she had to admit, duller before Nigel came to live with her. She enjoyed talking to him, telling him her problems and her joys. He seemed to listen intently when she talked to him, giving her wise looks, always agreeing with her own viewpoints. He was a satisfying companion.

Tally waited for Nigel to get halfway through his dinner, then told him she'd be back soon. He gave her a skeptical look.

"No, really, I will." At least she hoped she would.

He turned his tail end to her and left the room. She knew he'd finish his meal after she left. Nigel wasn't one to leave kibble uneaten.

Tomorrow was another big day and, after her late meal with Yolanda and Kevin, she needed to get home to ponder the job applications and, maybe, get a good night's sleep before another busy day at Tally's Olde Tyme Sweets tomorrow.

Tally walked quickly to Burger Kitchen through the soft night air, the warmth caressing her tired body and feeling so much better than the hot daytime air of August in this part of Texas.

Yolanda and Kevin were seated near the back and waved her over. Kevin gave her a smile through his au courant dark, scruffy beard. He was of medium height, unimposing and, as far as Tally could tell, a genuinely nice guy. He was, as usual, dressed all in black, black jeans and a black button-up shirt with the sleeves rolled up a few inches.

"I got you an iced tea," Yolanda said, taking a sip of her own.

Tally was thirsty from her two short, hot walks and gulped half the glass down. It tasted wonderful. The restaurant served their special blend, slightly sweet with a hint of peach flavoring.

"Now, what do you have?" Yolanda asked when Tally set her sweating glass on the paper coaster. "I saw you stick some papers in your purse. Any good prospects?"

"A few," Tally said. She fished them out of her purse and handed them to Yolanda. "Look them over and see what you think."

"Have you heard from your parents today?" Kevin asked.

The waiter brought them a basket of steaming breads and Kevin helped himself to a crusty roll.

Tally's roving musician/actor/dancer parents, Nancy and Bob Holt, were on their way home after many months on the road. They were coming in from Marrakesh in Morocco, where they had performed for a few days after their shows on the beach in Bali ended. The reception Tally was planning, with the help of Yolanda and Kevin, would be to celebrate their rare homecoming. She wanted it to be a special occasion for them. They had been gone for months, had never seen her shop, and she hoped they would be impressed. She had sold a successful bakery in Austin to buy her place here and she knew they didn't think it had been a good idea, even though this was their hometown and Tally had spent a good part of her childhood in this Texas Hill Country town.

"They're on a flight today, then stopping for a day in Spain and coming here from there," Tally said.

Kevin shook his head. "They sure gallivant around, don't they?"

"That's all they do. They never stay anywhere very long." Tally took a piece of steaming corn bread, her favorite, and started to butter it, letting it melt in before she took the first luscious bite.

"Y'all should put Cole to work since he's coming early," Yolanda said.

"He says he'll help me. We'll see if that happens."

"They're his parents, too. You can't blame him for wanting to pitch in."

"Wasn't this reception his idea?" Kevin asked, taking another warm roll.

"I guess it was," Tally said. "But I agreed to set it up. I thought he wouldn't be able to do much while he was building a sculpture in Albuquerque."

"I'm glad he'll be here," Kevin said. "We need all the hands we can get."

Tally drummed her fingers on the table, hoping that Kevin might be able to get more labor out of Tally's little brother than she would be likely to. Even though she was his big sister, she hadn't been able to boss him around for quite a few years now. Every single person in her family was the independent type.

She was half-dreading the reception. Her parents would fly in, get a few hours' sleep, and go straight to the party the next day—their choice. Tally knew they would be jet-lagged and the affair might be a dull flop. Then again, maybe she was wrong. They were so used to traveling, maybe they had conquered jet lag and would be ready to party. It was now Wednesday night, Cole would be here early Thursday, and her parents would arrive Friday. She had left the hiring of the help until almost too late, she knew. Actually, she hadn't even considered they would need help until Yolanda mentioned it. Yolanda was a great detail person, luckily.

"This has me rattled," Tally said. "I think I've let it get a lot bigger than I should have."

"You don't look a bit rattled," Kevin said with a smile. "You never do."

Tally knew she often looked cool, calm, and collected when she was a jangle of nerves inside. Maybe that was from being onstage from a young age. She was glad to be out of that life, but had to admit, the days when her parents used to give her and Cole parts in their acts had resulted in some useful takeaways. Cole and Yolanda were the two people on the planet who could always tell when she was upset and she was thankful for that. She would make the best of Cole being underfoot—no, not underfoot—being here and helping. Yes, that was it. Helping.

Her other worry was what this would do to her business. Missing a day of sales, and on a Saturday, would leave a big hole in her finances. She needed all of her income while her shop was still gathering steam and becoming known in the town.

"Let's talk about the reception," Yolanda said. "What are y'all going to serve?"

"My own products, of course," Tally answered. "I'll do some Mary Janes and Whoopie Pies. What else?"

Kevin said, "I think you should have your Clark Bars. I like that fudge with Baileys in it, too. I have a Petite Syrah that would be good with the fudge. If you do Twinkies, I'll bring some Riesling."

They discussed sweet treats and wine for a few more minutes until Tally changed the subject.

"Okay," she said, pointing to the three sheets of paper spread on the table. "What do you think of the applicants?"

Yolanda looked them over and held one up. "This one."

"Let me see." Kevin wiped his fingers so the butter from his roll wouldn't get on it. "Greer Tomson," he read. "She didn't graduate from high school. Is that a problem?"

"I'm not sure," Tally said. "The other two I liked are a bit younger. One is eighteen and the other one twenty. Greer has lots of work experience, so that might be good."

"Maybe too much," Yolanda said, frowning at the paper in her hand. "She seems to change jobs a lot."

"You're right," Kevin agreed, reaching for the paperwork from the other two and looking it over. "But she's the only one with retail experience."

"The good thing is," Tally said, "that I can try her out at the reception and then decide if I want to hire her to work in the store."

The server came and took their orders—hamburger, cheeseburger, and veggie burger.

"Back to the hired help," Kevin said, staying on point. "Are you just using one person at the reception?"

Tally gave it some thought. "What do both of you think? Do we need more?"

"What can you afford?" Yolanda asked. She was much better at managing money than Tally was. In fact, she helped Tally with the books in her shop when she couldn't make things balance.

"You probably know that better than I do." Tally laughed and Kevin chuckled.

"I think you're doing pretty darn well lately. You could hire all three, just for that day, then decide which two you want to keep."

Tally liked that idea. Like buying three pair of shoes, then returning the one or two pair that hurt her feet after an hour on the carpet at home. She decided to call all three and offer them jobs for Saturday. She would do it first thing in the morning.

As the three friends were winding up their dinner and waiting for the bill, a couple they all knew came through the door and were seated at a table near them. The pair looked like Jack Sprat and his wife, reversed. The woman was thin, with what looked like a perpetual frown on her creased face, which was topped by gray, short curls that always made Tally think of a mop. The man, in contrast, was bald, potbellied, and wore a jovial expression on his round face. Friendly eyes twinkled under his bushy eyebrows. The woman sat facing them, glanced in their direction, gathered her frown lines to new depths, loudly cleared her throat, then concentrated on her menu.

Kevin saw Tally's own frown and gave her a questioning look. "Later," she said.
"Yes, later," Yolanda added.

* * * *

Yolanda was surprised, but glad, when Kevin took her elbow and guided her out of the restaurant, just like they were an old married couple. She was beginning to look at him with a different view. He was older than she was, but seemed interested. She could do a lot worse.

When they were outside the restaurant Kevin asked again. "Do you not like the Abrahams?"

Yolanda started to answer, but Tally beat her to it. "Lennie is okay," she said, "but I can't stand his wife, Frances. She's had it in for my mother since I can remember."

"Tally's right," Yolanda said. "She finds something mean to say about Tally's mom every time they're in town."

"What's her problem?" Kevin asked. "I've heard only good things about your mom from several of my customers. They're excited she's going to be in town. I thought everyone liked her. Both of them, really."

They were walking toward Tally's house first, since she lived the closest. Yolanda wondered if Kevin was going to come to her place and stay for a while. Or overnight. The tree frogs were in full voice, their songs ringing above them through the night from the live oaks and crape myrtles that lined the streets. The air was deliciously cooler than the mid-nineties high of the day. The thermometer was heading for the high sixties and Yolanda wished she had a sweater on.

"That's one of the problems," Yolanda said. "Everyone likes Nancy, but hardly anyone likes Fran. Nancy is an old girlfriend of Fran's husband. Lennie still acts very friendly when he sees Nancy, which doesn't help anything."

Kevin pulled his head back and frowned. "Nancy is Mrs. Holt's first name? And she was a girlfriend of Mr. Abraham?"

Yolanda and Tally both nodded.

Kevin continued, "That must have been a long time ago. You're—what—in your thirties? So it had to be more than thirty years ago."

"Yes," Tally said. "Fran has been a thorn in my mom's side for their whole lives."

"One problem Fran has is competition," Yolanda said. "They're both performers, after all."

Yolanda had known Frances Abraham her whole life. Mrs. Abraham presently directed the local theater group and ruled it with an iron fist. To anyone she considered competition, she was extra-nasty. She had sent more than one aspiring starlet home in tears, wanting all the starring roles for herself. That became more and more problematic as she aged and her face became more and more set into permanent harsh lines that you could now see even beyond the stage. She had verbally attacked Yolanda's own sister, Violetta, so harshly and so often that Vi had dropped out of the one production she had tried out for. She'd been slated to have a starring role, too, but couldn't work under Fran. Yolanda remembered her little sister coming home in tears after every rehearsal until she quit.

"I've wondered before why Lennie puts up with her," Kevin said. "They come into Bear Mountain sometimes and whatever wine he picks out, she nixes. She's the boss."

"From working with them, I can tell you this," Yolanda answered. "He mostly ignores her. Just hammers the sets together and paints them and doesn't pay attention to what goes on in front of his scenery."

"I'd forgotten," Tally said to Yolanda. "You were in some of her plays, weren't you?"

"A while ago, when I was much younger. I didn't like working with her, but I stuck it out for a short time. Three productions one summer. I think most people who are in her productions put up with her because they love the stage."

"No one forgets the past in a small town like this," Kevin said.

"And she's not a bad director, just a limelight hog," Yolanda said.

"Too skinny for a hog," Kevin answered, and they all laughed.

They rounded the corner to Tally's block of East Shubert and she stopped. "It's a day early! He's here already!"

Her brother's Volvo sat in her driveway.

Chapter 2

"He was coming tomorrow, right?" Yolanda said.

"Right, he was. Nothing is ready. I'll see you two later." Tally took off, walking quickly, and Yolanda and Kevin headed toward Yolanda's, on West Shubert.

Tally composed herself walking the block to her front yard. There wasn't that much to do. She had to get out some linens for her brother to use on her couch, and a set of towels. If he had eaten, there wouldn't be dinner to make. She was exhausted and had been for days, getting ready for the gathering.

The quiet street, shaded by overhanging trees, soothed her. She strolled beneath them, hugging the curb since there were no sidewalks in her neighborhood. A radio played softly on the front porch she passed. She waved to the old man and he waved back, a ghostly motion in the darkness.

Maybe, she thought, it would be a good thing that her brother was here now. If she could put him to work, that is. They could use extra help. The trouble was, Cole pretty much did his own thing most of the time. Whenever Tally tried to influence his boorish behavior toward women, for example, nothing she did or said had any effect. Especially with his worst habit. He would date one woman, tire of her, then start dating Woman Number Two without officially breaking it off with Woman Number One. Most recently, he'd been seeing a young local woman named Dorella Diggs, when he had stayed briefly before taking off for Albuquerque to work on his commissioned statue. That was also when he had left Nigel with Tally. Another abandonment.

Tally had never had a cat before and was miffed when Cole assumed he could just dump the animal on her. It didn't take long before Tally got over that, since darling Nigel had won her over quickly.

She was curious to see if Cole would still be seeing Dorella this weekend. He would probably have to rush back to New Mexico after the reception. He didn't stay put for long.

As she walked up the porch steps, she heard Nigel let out a loud *ree-ow*. She pushed the door open. "What are you doing to the cat, Cole?" she teased.

"Hey, he heard you coming. He's greeting you. Have you left him all day with nothing to eat?"

"I'm fine, thanks. How are you doing? And I fed him about two hours ago."

Cole ignored her sarcasm. "It's a boring drive once you get away from Albuquerque. You should come up with me when I go back."

"Why would I like to go on a boring drive with you?"

They both stuck their tongues out at each other.

Nigel rubbed against her leg, purring, with a few trills added in, no doubt grateful she had fed him.

Tally kicked off her shoes and padded into the kitchen to check Nigel's bowls. His water was almost empty.

"Oh, sorry, big guy. You're running out of water."

Was Nigel raising his eyebrows at her? She thought he would probably roll his eyes if he could.

"I know. *Sorry* doesn't cut it." She filled his bowl at the faucet and set it on the floor.

Nigel sniffed it, took a tentative lap, then curled up on the floor. Maybe he was saving the water for later.

"How could I go with you to New Mexico, Cole?" she said, returning to the living room. "What would happen to my shop if I just flitted off whenever I felt like it?"

"Don't bite my head off, Sis." He gave her the Wounded Little Brother look.

She had to admit she'd sounded testy. She sat on the other end of the couch from Cole and curled up in the corner. "Sorry. But I really can't leave whenever I want. Right now I'm opening the shop seven days a week, except for this Saturday, to take advantage of the peak tourist season. I'll lay low after the beginning of the year when things slow down. Maybe we can do something together then."

"Tourists come here in August? I mean, I know they do. I can see the crowds. But I've always wondered why. It's so hot here. You'd think people would go somewhere cooler."

They had both grown up in Fredericksburg, but neither had ever viewed the town with an entrepreneurial eye as children.

"Christmas shopping, of course," Tally said. "We merchants try to make them believe they need to shop for months and months. Merchants everywhere do that. And most people who come here to Fredericksburg believe it, I think."

"I know you're right. The Christmas Shop does good business year-round, doesn't it? I remember that from when I was here."

The television was on, muted. He had probably muted it when she came in. Out of the corner of her eye, Tally caught an ad for a man running for mayor. He was unfamiliar. "Who's that?" she asked. "Do you know?"

"How would I know? I just got here."

It was his turn to snap at her, but now, Tally figured, they were even. "I've never seen his ads before. I wonder if he's new around town."

Nigel strolled in from the kitchen and hopped up beside Tally, setting up a rumbling, purring racket.

"How's the party going?" Cole asked. "You got everything under control?"

"I wish! I've interviewed people until I'm cross-eyed and have come up with exactly three who I think might work." Tally was worn out. She wanted to stay on her soft, secondhand navy blue couch until morning, it was so comfy. Nigel looked as if he agreed with her and would like to do that, too.

"Interviewed for what? For the sweet shop?"

"To help serve the reception, first of all. Then, if any of them work out, I'll hire one or two for the store."

"What about Dorella?"

"What do you mean?"

"She'd be great in your store."

"Cole, I interviewed people who applied for the job. I didn't get an application from her."

"Maybe she didn't know about it."

Tally bit her tongue to keep from saying what she was thinking. "I can't read people's minds and go looking for them. Does that make sense?"

Nigel licked her arm. Did he approve of Dorella?

"Okay." Cole gave her a sullen look, then brightened. "Hey, you have anything to eat?"

Of course he was hungry. She'd been so comfy.

Before she pushed herself up to see if there was anything to feed to her brother, Cole's phone chirped.

"Hey, it's Dorella," he said, rising from the couch. "Maybe she'll feed me." He went to the kitchen to take the call.

She had to assume he was still seeing her. That was a good sign. Maybe he was settling down and not flitting between women as often as usual.

When he came back, he said that Dorella was coming over to pick him up.

"She's really buying you dinner?" Tally wondered if anything was still open this late.

"I'm buying, Sis. I was just kidding."

"Where you going?"

"Otto's is still open. She doesn't have to work her day job tomorrow."

"So you'll be late coming back here? Don't wake me up when you get in, okay? I have to go to the shop early tomorrow."

"How come?" Cole smoothed his hair in front of the mirror that hung by Tally's front door.

"I'm going to call in the three women I want to hire before the shop opens. I want to give them some instructions and make sure they can work on Saturday."

A few minutes later, the doorbell rang. Cole tucked his lips in and checked his teeth in the mirror. He smiled at his reflection and opened the door to let Dorella Diggs in, still wearing his big grin.

Nigel jumped down from the couch and greeted the newcomer with a chirp and a headbutt to her leg. Dorella reached down to stroke his broad back.

Tally wished she had Dorella's soft blond curls. They nestled around her heart-shaped face perfectly. If he was going by looks, no wonder Cole was still with her. But she was also likeable. Her only flaw known to Tally was an occasional flare-up of her quick temper.

"You have flowers in my vase," Dorella said, straightening up and looking at the carnations in the blue vase on Tally's shelf. Dorella worked at Burger Kitchen, but also made pottery and had given the handsome handmade vase to Tally the last time Cole was in town.

"I love it," Tally said, truthfully. "Anything looks good in it."

"See you sometime tomorrow," Cole said, herding Dorella out the door. "Bye, Tally."

Nigel climbed into Tally's lap and they settled in to watch some television before she got too sleepy to keep her eyes open. Not for too long, though. She did have to get in early tomorrow.

* * * *

Tally called all three prospects first thing Thursday morning from her office in Tally's Olde Tyme Sweets and they all said they would show up in a few minutes. That was a good sign, she hoped. Her shop was due to open at ten, in about forty-five minutes, which gave her enough time to give them some preliminary instructions.

Lily Vale was the first to arrive and Molly Kelly came in a few minutes later. They were both young. Lily had just graduated from high school and Molly had recently dropped out of her freshman year of college. On her application, she had indicated that a family situation dictated she move back home.

Tally met them at the front door, unlocked it to let them in, ringing the chimes as they entered, and showed them into the kitchen behind the salesroom. They all pulled out stools and sat at the island. Tally rested her elbows on the cool taupe granite countertop.

"Thank you for coming in this morning on such short notice." If they hadn't been able to come this morning, she still had another day before the event. "First of all, I want you to know what my products are because that's what you'll be serving at the party. Can y'all both still work all day Saturday?"

They both nodded.

"The reception is for your parents?" Lily asked, opening her already large brown eyes wider with her question. She was thin and graceful, with long reddish hair that shone in the warm sunlight coming through the paned windows on the rear wall of the kitchen.

"Yes, they haven't been home for a long time. A lot of people in the town are coming to see them. They won't be here long, so I have to squeeze this in."

"How come?" Molly asked. She was the opposite of Lily in appearance. Her hair was dark and very short, and her eyes a brilliant blue. "I mean, how come they're gone all the time?"

"They're performers, musicians and dancers. They take their act all over the world."

"Sounds like they're doing well," Lily said. "I'm a dancer, too."

"Do you dance locally?" Tally asked.

"I've done some at the Palace, that place that Frances Abraham runs."

"That's rad," Molly said, giving Lily a high five.

Tally didn't have much time for chitchat, so she brought them back to the topic. "Here's a list of what we'll serve at the reception." She set a printout before them so they could look it over.

"What are Mary Janes?" Molly asked.

"They're candies from Boston," Tally told her. "They're mostly sugar, molasses, and peanut butter."

"Mm. Sounds good," Lily said.

"Molasses?" Molly made a face. "That stuff is nasty."

"Okay," Tally said to her, keeping her voice level. "On Saturday, you need to keep your opinions to yourself. I want you all to know what the products are, in case anyone asks—"

"Just don't tell them if they're any good or not, right?" Molly said.

After a beat, Tally replied, "Right." Had she made a mistake choosing Molly?

Tally went over the list of goodies she would serve: Twinkies, Clark Bars, Whoopie Pies, Baileys Truffle Fudge, Mary Janes, and Mallomars. She thought six different choices would give everyone enough variety. Kevin had chosen four wines, two red and two white, to complement them.

"The Clark Bars and the Mary Janes contain peanut butter, so if someone has an allergy and asks, tell them not to eat those two."

"Did you make all of these?" Molly asked. "Here?" She looked around the kitchen and Tally wondered if she was waiting for candy to emerge, fully formed, from the countertops.

Tally assured her that she did.

"Why are you serving Twinkies? You can't make those."

"Yes, I can. And I do make them. They're my own version. Better than the commercial kind. At least, I think so." Tally smiled at them, proud of her creations.

"How much are we allowed to eat?"

Suppressing a frown, Tally answered. "When the party's done, I'll hand out some leftovers."

"Well," Molly said, "can we at least drink the wine?"

Tally caught herself before that frown went too far. "Not while you're working."

Molly made a face and shrugged.

A knock sounded on the front door. Tally hoped that was Greer. She dashed to the front to let her in.

"Good morning." Greer gave a big smile that drew attention to how red her lipstick was. She had a narrow face and curly brunette hair twisted up into a messy bun with a butterfly clip at the back of her head. She didn't say anything about being very late.

"We're just about finished, but there are a few more things to go over with Lily and Molly. I'll try to catch you up when we're done, if there's time."

"Sounds cool."

Tally tried not to be aggravated by the woman. She was older than the other two, near thirty. She had to remember that her age meant Greer might be more experienced than the other two, which would be an advantage.

There was another knock at the front door. As Greer disappeared into the kitchen, Tally turned to find Allen Wendt peering in. She ran to unlock the door once again, and noticed his white pickup idling at the curb. They had made a few tentative tries at a relationship, but Tally didn't know where it was going at this point. She didn't even know, from one day to the next, whether he'd still be living in this town or not. He'd drifted in a while ago and she expected him to drift out again some day.

"Hey, I just need to tell you," he said, "I can't make your party on Saturday."

"I'm sorry to hear that." He hadn't positively said he would when she'd asked him, but he must have been planning on it.

"Yeah, I took a new job. I'm pretty pumped about it."

"Good for you." He'd been picking up odd jobs and she knew he hadn't been getting many lately.

"Yeah, I'm driving a truck. Long-haul."

The smells of sunshine and soap emanated from him. Tally breathed in the pleasant scents and stepped a bit closer.

"You think you'll like that?" she asked. "Don't you have to get a special license?"

"I did. I passed the test and I have to be ready to start my first route any day now. They told me Friday or Saturday."

That kind of work might suit him. "You should enjoy that. Being on the move. You don't like to stay put, do you?" He had likened himself to a tumbleweed once and it was an apt description.

He shrugged. "I'll see. Hey, good luck with the party."

They hadn't progressed to a kiss good-bye. Tally didn't know if they ever would, at this rate.

She got back to training the prospective helpers. They all three had a chance to walk around balancing trays with plates and glasses on them. Tally planned for them to use the trays when they circulated among the guests, offering them wine and sweet treats. After that, Tally sat with Greer and went over the list of what would be served and explained some of them.

"The part about peanut butter is important for people with allergies," she said. "So remember that." She wasn't sure Greer was taking all of this in, since she had only glanced at the list of candies.

After she asked all three of them to come in Friday night to help with last-minute preparations, she shooed them out and opened her store. The onslaught of sweet treat buyers made her wish she had kept one of them to help her out for the day. But she stuck to her resolve to try them all out on Saturday before she decided who to hire for the shop.

Chapter 3

The rest of Thursday and all day Friday flew by for Tally in a flurry of baking, wrapping, cleaning, and smiling the whole time at the thought of all the wares she was selling. She worked late hours both days to make sure she had made enough food for the reception, as well as to keep up with the bustling business she was doing. The amount of business both days made her wish she could continue the momentum and not close on Saturday. Over and over, she told herself, *It's only one day.*

Friday at 7:00, after the store closed at the usual time, Lily and Molly showed up promptly and Greer fifteen minutes later. She had made enough of some of the confections, but needed to make more Clark Bars, more Twinkies, and a few more Whoopie Pies. Molly jumped at the chance to help with the Twinkies. Lily got instructions on how to make the boiled Clark Bars. They were a simple candy of sugar, corn syrup, peanut butter, and rice cereal, frosted with chocolate chips. And Greer was put to work on the Whoopie Pies. Tally thought she might be a slower worker and she only needed one more half batch of those.

Tally had just come into the kitchen from her office, where she had gone to check on her orders for next week, when she heard Lily talking to the other two.

"This is so much fun," Lily said as she swirled the peanut butter into the boiled sugars.

She was glad to hear Lily say that. The others didn't answer her, though.

"Are you having fun?" Tally asked Molly.

"I dunno. I guess so. It's not as much fun to make Twinkies as I thought it would be."

"How about you, Greer?" Tally asked.

"What?" She'd been staring into the distance, holding a spreader full of Whoopie Pie filling, marshmallow crème, butter, and powdered sugar, and dripping some onto the counter.

Tally refrained from rolling her eyes. "I asked if you're having a good time."

"Well, I'm on a job, right? So it's working, not fun. When do we get our break?"

"Greer, you're only here for three hours tonight." Tally glanced at the clock on the kitchen wall, the one with the chubby, aproned baker using his arms to tell the time. It was 9:00. "If you can't make it another hour, take a short break. You've gotten a lot done, all of you."

Molly and Greer headed out the back door. Tally hadn't expected that. Were they going somewhere? Lily looked puzzled, too, and kept working. Tally regretted saying they could have a break when they came in twenty minutes later, both reeking of tobacco smoke.

Maybe it was too early, but Tally felt she might have to cross Greer and Molly off the list of who to hire on at the store.

* * * *

Tally's parents got in extra-late Friday night, due to a delayed flight, a missed one, and a rebooking. Everyone was happy that their luggage made it through with them. Cole picked them up and offered to move to a motel, but Nancy and Bob insisted on staying in one so they wouldn't displace their son. In spite of the late hour, they insisted on seeing Tally's place.

Friday night, Tally was ready to leave, having gotten the kitchen cleaned up after the flurry of preparation that had gone on until ten, when Cole called and caught her up on their parents' arrival.

"Yes, bring them by," she said. "It'll never look better than it does right now."

"We're on our way," Cole said.

When they finally gazed upon her store, her parents were suitably impressed.

"Tally," her mother said, eyeing the pink and lilac swirled walls and the wide-planked flooring in the salesroom, "this is terrific. It's so attractive." She spun around, taking in the shelves, the gleaming candy display case— now empty—and tilting her head up to admire the mason jar light fixtures. "I didn't know you had such decorating talent."

Tally laughed. "If my sweet shop fails, maybe I could do decor instead."

They inspected the kitchen, too. Tally stifled a few yawns, noticing how alert and awake her parents were after their long trip. She was too tired to figure out what time it was in the zone they had just come from, in Morocco and Spain.

Tally went with Cole to drop them off at the Sunday House Inn and Suites, a hotel very close to the business district. The hotel was named after the distinctive Sunday Houses that the town was known for. They were now quite expensive and Yolanda lived in one of them.

They had said they would show up early for the afternoon reception, and Tally knew they would. She marveled at their stamina, after flying halfway around the world. But that was nothing new to them.

* * * *

Saturday morning dawned bright and sunny and hot, as usual. When Dorella Diggs came into the shop, midmorning, setting off the soft door chime, Tally and Cole were almost finished moving the round tables to where Tally wanted them. On a normal business day, they were heaped with boxes of her products, but today they would hold wine, stacks of small plates and napkins, and large plates of unwrapped candies, set out for the guests. Dorella got to work setting things out and took great care arranging everything just so. Tally was glad an artist was handling that part of the affair. They looked beautiful, enticing. Cole had come over with Tally, earlier, to help out and was actually being useful. Yolanda, wrapped up in flowing aquas and chartreuses, breezed in soon after Dorella, bringing the chairs Tally had rented for the occasion.

* * * *

Yolanda started unfolding the rental chairs as she talked to Tally. She knew she had to warn her about what was coming. "Violetta is going to be here to help," she said. Violetta was her younger sister, who lived in Dallas. "She should arrive in a few minutes."

"She's coming up just for this?" Tally asked.

"Not exactly. She had planned to come up already."

"She was just here, wasn't she? A week or so ago?"

Yolanda looked away. "Here's the thing—Vi told me, but our parents don't know yet. She has a girlfriend."

"Like in, girlfriend girlfriend?"

"Yes, like that. I always wondered why she had never dated, and after she talked to me a couple of days ago, now I know. I'm very happy for her, that she found out who she is and that she found someone who, she says, she loves and who also loves her. But…"

"Your parents don't know," Tally guessed.

Tally knew the Bella family well. Yolanda knew she could count on Tally to buffer the coming confrontation. Yolanda's parents were strict, old-fashioned and, in many ways, intolerant of anyone different.

"Exactly," Yolanda answered. "Eden—her name is Eden Casey—wanted to meet our family this weekend and Vi said okay. So she's thinking maybe she'll tell them quietly at the reception, in public, where they can't have such a bad reaction."

"I suppose that might work." Tally sounded doubtful.

"I hope there isn't a scene at your event, but I don't think they'll make one out in the open, where everyone can see them. Do you?"

"It should be all right. If they do, well…there probably isn't a better way to do this."

"They'll both be here in a few minutes."

"Both of them?" Tally asked. "Good. I'll get to meet Eden before the party starts."

When Violetta and Eden got to the shop twenty minutes later, Yolanda saw Tally hurry toward the front to greet them. Violetta took charge right inside the door.

"Everyone," Violetta said, raising her voice to be heard over the chatter and noise of setting up, "I want you to meet my friend, Eden. She's up for the weekend from Dallas to meet my family."

Eden Casey had red hair, a broad Irish face, and a huge, warm smile. Everyone returned her smile and nodded.

Violetta started to introduce Eden to everyone. "This is my sister, Yolanda," she said in her usual soft, musical voice. "And this is her friend, Tally, and Tally's brother, Cole. And…" Violetta looked a question at Cole.

Tally jumped in when she saw Violetta floundering. She had no idea who Dorella was. "Eden, I'd like you to meet Dorella, Cole's friend who is helping out today." She was reluctant to call Dorella his girlfriend, given Cole's history of dumping women so often, even if that's exactly what she was. For the moment.

"It's nice to meet all of you," Eden said. "I'm very happy to be here. Vi told me you're throwing a party because your parents are in town for a few days, Tally. This looks fantastic. Is there anything I can do to help?"

"I think we're mostly ready," Tally said. "Mom called just a few minutes ago and they're on their way over."

"I hope some people show up," Cole said. "We practically invited the whole town."

"We *did* invite the whole town," Tally said. "We put an announcement in the local paper."

Ten minutes went by while everyone fiddled with the streamers, straightened plates, and flicked invisible flecks of dust from the tables. Tally started getting nervous. No one else was here yet. What if no one came? There were lots of people in Fredericksburg who knew her parents, but hadn't seen them in a long time. She had assumed they would want to see them, but maybe they didn't.

Just in time, all three of the young women Tally had hired to serve walked into the shop. She quickly gave them smocks, two lilac and one pink, to match the walls of the shop, and was glad she had shown them where everything was the day before. By the time the three came out of the kitchen with some trays for circulating, guests were starting to pour in.

Tally relaxed. It would be fine. People were showing up.

* * * *

About an hour into the party, Tally took a moment to lean against the candy counter and take a breath. Her parents were chatting with Mrs. Gerg, Tally's landlady and neighbor. Kevin Miller had arrived and gone straight to check on the wines he'd brought over earlier. Yolanda swooped in on him and introduced her sister and her sister's girlfriend. People were clustered in groups, chatting and, to all appearances, having a good time.

Fran and Len Abraham had recently shown up, making a dramatic entrance, as befitted theater people. Some other theater people were already there. Some were probably associates of Fran and Len and some knew Nancy and Bob from their local performances years ago.

The shop got warmer and warmer with the noisy crowd, so Tally nudged the AC to be a notch colder. Welcome cool air spilled out of the vents immediately.

Tally's phone buzzed in her pocket. A glance showed her it was Allen as she answered it.

"Hey, I just wanted to see how your deal was going."

That was nice! "I'm tired and I'll sleep soundly tonight, but it's going well. Tons of people showed up and I think my parents are having a good time. Lots of old friends and people who've known them for a long time are here."

"Glad you're doing okay. Just...wanted to check in."

"I'm glad you did. When are you coming home? Do you know?"

"Yeah, well, not really. I could pick up an extra load. Maybe. Don't know yet. I'll call you when I get back."

Tally smiled as she tucked her phone into her pocket.

A woman named Shiny Peth had arrived just after the Abrahams. Tally knew her vaguely and noticed she seemed to be stuck to Len, batting her false eyelashes and running a hand down her admirable model-thin body. Tally wondered if she was thinking others would think she was smoothing her dress. But no one thought that, of course. The woman was showing off her perfect body.

Lily stopped and whispered to Tally, "See that woman with Lennie? Fran blackballed her from the theater." She was talking about Shiny Peth, the one Tally had been glancing at as she made her way around the room.

Tally could see why. Shiny was a huge threat to Fran, judging from Len's reciprocal flirting and Fran's sour looks at both of them. As Tally and Lily watched, Fran turned away from them and went over to Bob Holt. Tally thought she was flirting with him just as outrageously as Shiny was flirting with Len, but with much less success. Her father was a one-woman man, Tally was sure. Anyway, how could Len put up with anyone with such a grating, nasal voice as Shiny had? It probably carried onstage, but it was annoying up close.

"I wonder if Fran would be drinking so much wine if Shiny weren't here," Lily whispered, then headed toward Fran to give her a fresh glass from the tray she balanced gracefully.

Another theater person, Ionia Goldenberger, stood chatting with Nancy, Tally's mother. They both went way back, having started together when they were both very young in local theater. Ionia had been active on the stage for years until Fran recently took over as director. Tally wondered if her mother's old friend resented Fran's position. She knew from her mother that Ionia would have made an excellent director.

Tally studied her mother, thinking she looked pale. Did she look distressed? Was she ill? As she was watching, her mother hurried into the kitchen. Tally followed and saw her dash into the bathroom.

"Are you okay?" she asked when her mother came out.

"Just a little queasy," she said. "Do you have any ginger ale? I don't think I can do any more wine right now." She looked flushed and perspiration dotted her forehead and upper lip.

Tally got her a Sprite and she seemed to feel better after a few small sips.

Soon after Tally followed her mother out of the kitchen, Mr. and Mrs. Bella, the parents of Yolanda and Violetta, came into the shop. Tally looked around to see where Violetta and Eden were. They were at the opposite corner of the room. Yolanda was chatting in a cluster of people near the front door. After stopping for them to greet both Bob and Nancy Holt, she stepped out of the group and steered her parents toward her sister for the planned confrontation.

Tally was too far away and the buzz of the crowd too great to allow her to hear the conversation, but she could follow it. The older Bellas nodded to Eden as they were introduced. Violetta held her shoulders high and taut. She opened her mouth, closed it, pressed her lips together, then began to talk, a worried look on her soft, young face. Tally knew she was telling her parents the news. That their daughter—their paragon of virtue, the one they always compared Yolanda to unfavorably, the daughter who was following her father into the family's real estate business, and their hope for future grandchildren—preferred women. That would be hard, Tally knew, for them to accept.

Tally had to wonder if this had been the best way to tell them. Maybe the public-place idea wasn't such a good one.

Mr. Bella drew back two steps from the young women, his face blank. Mrs. Bella tilted her head, a puzzled look on her face. Then Mr. Bella lowered his thick eyebrows and sneered, overcome with a look of thunderous anger. He roughly grabbed his wife's arm and hurried her through the people and out the front door.

Yolanda, Violetta, and Eden looked at each other, deflated. Soon they were mingling with the townspeople and Tally relaxed. At least there hadn't been a loud scene here. That would come later, she predicted.

Lily collected the empty glasses of a couple Tally didn't know and made her way through the crowd to get replacements or refill them. After a second or two, Tally recognized the man as the person she'd seen on television running for mayor. She assumed the woman was his wife. Molly wended her way from group to group, offering everyone more Clark Bars and Twinkies. Greer emerged from the kitchen with some Whoopie Pies on her tray and headed for Len. Both he and Shiny declined them, so she offered some to Fran. Bob had just walked away from her. Fran knocked back her new glass of wine and piled some Whoopie Pies onto her plate.

Then Greer headed for the senior Holts, who were now standing close together. Bob looked like he was hovering over his pale wife. Greer paused on her way as Fran—Whoopie Pies and wine already quickly demolished—

approached Nancy. Ionia saw her coming and turned her back to block Fran, but Fran barged ahead. Everyone knew that Fran should stay away from Nancy.

"I heard about your latest performances," Fran said to Nancy, her voice loud, drunk, and grating.

"That's nice." Nancy swayed in place. She looked uncertain if that was a compliment or not. "We've had some good runs lately."

"No wonder." Fran's voice got even louder. "That's my material you're using. You know you stole everything you use from me."

Nancy gaped at the woman, holding Ionia's arm for support. "You're crazy. Bob and I have always written all of our acts. Our music, lyrics, choreography, everything." Nancy's voice was louder now and the woman knew how to project. Both of these women did. "I could ruin you professionally in this town, you know. You'd better not accuse me of anything like that ever again, or—"

Tally squeezed her eyes shut. *Now* there was a scene.

"Or what?" Fran shouted. "What will you do?"

"Excuse me," Nancy said, her voice weak. Bob had put his arm around her shoulder, protectively, when the confrontation started. Nancy turned to him and spoke for a moment. They both headed for Tally, leaving Fran sputtering in place.

"You just wait until I tell everyone about what I know," Fran screeched after them.

"Tally," her mom said. "I feel awful. My mouth is so dry and I'm—I'm—" She looked around in confusion, like she didn't know where she was. "Can you take me to your place?"

"I'll take you, poppet," her dad said. He felt his wife's forehead with the back of his hand. "She's burning up. Something's very wrong." He shot an angry glare at Fran, who returned it.

"My car's out back, Dad," Tally said. "Go ahead and use that." She got her car keys from her purse in the locked drawer of her office and gave them to him.

Cole and their father took Nancy to Tally's house and Cole returned in a few minutes without him. The party was still in full swing, honoring her parents—going on without them.

"Is Dad coming back?" she asked her brother.

"I don't think so. Mom is getting sicker by the minute. She's weak and clammy and confused."

"We should wind this up, then," she said.

Tally didn't see Greer or Molly anywhere and went to the kitchen to find them. Molly was thumbing her phone in front of the sink.

"What are you doing in here?" Tally asked. "And where's Greer?"

"She left. She said she was sick. I had some texts I needed to answer."

"She left and didn't tell me?"

"She was sick," Molly repeated, as if that was a reasonable thing.

"You do not need to answer texts while you're working. The party is probably ending soon."

"Already? How come?"

"My parents have both had to leave. You would know that if you'd been out there where you should be. Now put your phone away. Start gathering things and clean up."

She followed Molly through the kitchen door to see everyone gathered around someone on the floor. After she shoved her way through the knot of people, she saw Fran curled up on the floor, twitching and clutching her stomach, moaning piteously. Tally looked around for Fran's husband and didn't see him.

"Len!" she called, panic tightening her vocal cords and making her voice high and squeaky. "Len Abraham!"

"He's out front," someone said. One of the guests brought him inside, Shiny trailing behind them.

Everyone started speaking at once.

"You have to take her to the hospital."

"She was fine a minute ago."

"What's the matter with her?"

Kevin asked Tally what was wrong with her mother. "Do they have the same thing?"

"I don't know. Mom has a fever. I think we'll have to take her to the emergency room, too."

Len got Fran to their car out front, with the help of a couple of other men, and headed for the hospital. Tally watched the taillights depart, sad that the party was ending so badly.

Most of the people started to leave. After the Abrahams were gone, Tally, Cole, and Dorella shooed the last of them out, locked up, and drove back to Tally's house. It didn't take them more than a minute to decide to take Nancy to the hospital.

Nancy was in such bad shape by the time they got to the emergency room that the nurses took her in to a cubicle right away, ahead of a couple of sick-looking children and a man who appeared to have a broken arm.

It didn't take the doctor long to figure out what Nancy had after Bob told him where they'd been, Thailand, Bali, and Morocco most recently.

"It's most likely that she has dengue fever," he said. "I'll test her, but the results will take several days. I'd like to keep her here overnight on an IV to make sure she's getting enough fluid. We'll treat her with Tylenol and she'll probably be able to leave in the morning. Mr. Holt, we'll get a cot so you can spend the night with her if you'd like."

"Yes, please," Tally's dad said. "I'd very much like that."

Cole offered to bring some things to them from their luggage.

Tally wasn't sure what dengue fever was, but it sounded exotic. Leave it to her mother to get an exotic disease.

* * * *

Early the next morning, before Tally got out of bed, her phone rang. She groped for it on her nightstand and opened it to hear a familiar voice.

"Tally," Detective Jackson Rogers said, "can you come down to the station and talk to me about what happened at your place yesterday?"

Her heart hammered and her neck hairs stood on end at the flat, cold, serious tone of his voice. He was speaking officially. She recognized that tone. "You mean Fran and Mom? Why? What's wrong?"

"Frances Abraham passed away at the hospital a short time ago and I need to talk to you about what she ate and drank."

Chapter 4

Detective Rogers told Tally to let the crime-scene people into her shop and then come to the station. After the guests had left the night before, she had rushed to the hospital to see how her mother was doing, leaving the cleanup until morning. She had intended to go in early the next day, before anyone else got there, but not this early.

Now, Sunday morning, after she unlocked her shop for them, the crime-scene team swept through the kitchen efficiently, photographing everything, then collecting the serving platters from the counter where they waited to be washed, even taking the trash bags full of scraps, disposable cups, napkins, and empty wine bottles.

Tally felt queasy watching them. The detective called her again, asking her when she was coming in. She left the forensics people, still working, and drove through the coolish early morning to the police station at the edge of town. She hoped she wouldn't have to spend too much time there, since she needed to open her shop. She *had* hoped to see her mother first, but that might not happen. Saturday had been a day of lost business and she couldn't afford to lose Sunday, too.

There were times when she enjoyed being with Detective Jackson Rogers, but being questioned at the police station was not one of them. When the misunderstanding about Yolanda had been cleared up a few weeks ago, Tally had hoped to see if a relationship would develop between her and the handsome gray-eyed detective. So far, nothing.

Seated in an interrogation room and looking into those eyes, she realized this wasn't an occasion to further their rapport. Those eyes, which could look soft and dreamy on occasion, were now gunmetal cold and the detective was all business.

"Thanks for coming in," he said, taking the chair across from her. Another policeman was sitting beside him. She recognized Officer Edwards, a large, beefy uniformed officer with a badly pockmarked face.

Tally started in before Jackson could say anything else. "You think Fran was poisoned?"

The detective narrowed his eyes at her. "What makes you say that?"

"You said you needed to talk about what she ate and drank. And that she has died. It's not a stretch to think you're suspecting food poisoning."

"Did you see what she ate and drank?"

All business today, of course. She liked it much better when they met for coffee and chatted. Would that happen again?

"She drank a lot, but it was the same thing everyone else was drinking, bottled wine from Kevin's Bear Mountain Vineyards."

Tally had written down as many names as she could remember, knowing from experience that he would ask her who had been there. "Here's everyone I can remember." She unfolded the paper and pushed it across the table to him.

He looked at it briefly, nodded, and stuck it between the pages of his notebook. "How closely did you observe Mrs. Abraham during the party?"

"I had a lot to do. I couldn't watch her all night."

"Who did you see her with?"

Tally cast her mind back and could only recall a few. "She came with her husband Lennie, of course. Then Shiny Peth joined them and Fran... went over to where my dad was. Then she went to my mom, who was with Ionia, and started yelling at her. Fran was very drunk, from what I could tell. Ionia tried to run interference, but Fran plowed her way in."

"Anyone else?"

"Probably, but I can't recall any more. There were people there I didn't know. We put a notice in the paper and the whole town was invited."

He scribbled something on his notepad so illegibly she couldn't read it upside down.

"How about what she ate?" he asked.

"No one else was poisoned by anything, were they? All the food was made in my kitchen. You can't tell people she got food poisoning from my treats."

"Do you know, specifically, what things she ate?"

Tally closed her eyes to remember if she'd seen Fran eating anything in particular. She remembered that she had eaten a pile of Whoopie Pies just before she came over to confront her mother. "Whoopie Pies. Probably a lot of other things, too, but she definitely ate a pile of Whoopie Pies."

"I hear that your father was close to Fran for a lot of the night."

"What's that supposed to mean? Who told you that? I don't think he was near her for more than a few minutes."

"Who did you see her with last?"

"I told you, she was arguing with my mother. That was just before she collapsed. Maybe Fran got dengue fever from Mom."

"Your mother has dengue fever? When did that happen?" He leaned back in his chair. It had a squeak that needed oil or something.

"She started to feel sick at the reception and had to leave. She probably felt bad before that and thought she could get through it, but she ended up going to the hospital after the party." Tally was beginning to feel sick from this interview, too. "She got it in Asia."

"No one mentioned that."

"How many people have you talked to? Everyone knows she was sick. It was her party and she had to leave it."

"We're questioning everyone who was there."

"Who told you my dad was sticking close to Fran? Or that she had food poisoning? People don't suddenly die of that."

"No, they don't die of food poisoning suddenly. They can die of poisoned food, though."

"Poisoned food? Someone poisoned some of my food?" That didn't make sense. "No one else got sick from it. Are you sure she didn't have dengue fever?"

Tally drummed her fingers on the edge of his desk, then made herself stop.

The detective said, "I don't think people suddenly die of that an hour after exposure, do you? I may be wrong, but I don't think you can catch it from being with an infected person either. Don't you get it from mosquitoes?"

Tally could see she needed to do some research about what her mother had, and ask the doctor a lot of questions. "I can't tell you much more. I was busy running around making sure everyone was having a good time and had enough to eat and drink." And tracking down her hired helpers. "Can I go now?"

The two law enforcement officers exchanged looks and the detective nodded. "For now. I might have more questions later. If you remember more about what Mrs. Abraham ate, let me know right away."

Tally promised to do that and sped back to her shop. The detective had told her the team was done collecting evidence and her premises were released. She needed to make sure everything was in order for business today.

She would like to know who told Detective Rogers her dad had been hanging around Fran. He hadn't. On the contrary, he'd been trying to get away from her. Fuming about her interrogation, she jerked her car to a stop behind her shop and stomped into the kitchen. It didn't look too bad. Until she looked more closely at the countertops. They would all have to be cleaned. Faint gray powder covered many of the surfaces, not just the countertops. She needed extra help today more than ever.

As she dialed Lily Vale's number, her hands shook from anger and adrenaline so that she could hardly press the keys. Fortunately, Lily answered immediately and said she could start work that morning, could be there in twenty minutes. Tally glanced at the clock. It was half an hour until she should open. That would be perfect.

She slumped back in her desk chair, wondering if she should call the other two, Greer and Molly. They had all done good work at the reception, mostly. If Greer were sick, she wouldn't be able to come in today, though. Maybe she could get Lily full-time and the other two could relieve each other working part-time. She opened her desk drawer and got out an employee agreement for Lily, then called Molly.

* * * *

Tally was beginning to relax. It was after 1:30 in the afternoon and things had gone smoothly all day. She and Lily had worked in the kitchen right after opening and Molly had handled sales. When it got busier and there were plenty of products on the shelves, all three of them started selling.

Midmorning, the door chimed and Tally looked up to see who had come in. She had just finished waiting on a family from Colorado vacationing in the Hill Country, and was surprised to see Greer Tomson standing inside the door with a dour look on her face.

"Greer," Tally said. "Hi. Are you feeling better?"

A look of confusion flitted across Greer's face. "Yes, much better." She frowned. "Why are they working here? You didn't call me?"

She was just checking up now? Tally looked for signs of illness. She didn't look sick. Her color was good. "I wanted to give you time to get well. Sick people can't work in a place selling edibles."

Greer nodded slowly, thinking about that. "Okay."

"Come back to my office and we can talk," Tally said. Once there, she told Greer to have a seat and she sat behind her desk. "Do you want to work part-time? You and Molly can alternate days." She had given Molly a part-time employee agreement, hoping to try both of them out for a week or so, maybe longer.

Greer looked away and frowned. "I guess. Maybe I could get more hours? Later? I'm on my own and I need the job. My parents are both dead."

"I'm so sorry, Greer. Maybe I can help you. Can you come to work tomorrow? You'll have to be on time." Tally assumed that Greer would come in late, since she had so far. But if she were working regularly, Tally could always hope.

Greer brightened. "Yes, I can do that. Tomorrow. Okay." She got up to leave.

"Wait," Tally said, catching her arm. "You need to be here at nine-thirty. We open at ten and you have to help get things ready."

Her smile deepened. "Thanks so much. I really need this job."

Chapter 5

Yolanda looked up from the large basket she was finishing for a neighborhood block party that evening, as something darkened the large display window of Bella's Baskets. She saw one of Tally's servers from the reception. The young woman was slumped against the front window of her shop. When she turned her head, Yolanda saw tears on her face. She pictured the résumés she'd seen, but couldn't quite remember the young woman's name. Grace? Gloria? Gina?

"I'll be right back," she said to Raul, her young, handsome part-time assistant, and went out to see if she could help the poor woman.

The young woman looked up when she came out and Yolanda saw the look of sadness on her face. "Can I help you? Grace, is it?"

Shaking her head, Greer answered, "Greer. I don't think you can help me."

Yolanda wondered if Tally had fired her already. Or had not hired her. "What's the matter?"

"Everything."

"Tell me. Maybe I know what you're going through."

"Has your dad ever gone to prison?" Greer looked at her directly for the first time, her eyes glistening with tears. Her words were a challenge. Belligerent.

"No." Yolanda had to admit that, in spite of her father's other faults, being in prison wasn't one of them. "Come inside and I'll get you a Coke."

Greer followed her into the shop and accepted a chilled can from Yolanda's flower cooler, which doubled as a soda refrigerator. "Thanks." She gulped it down noisily.

"Did your father just get sent to…prison?"

"No, he's been there for years."

"What about your mother? Is she...in the picture?"

"I guess. She can't work or anything."

Greer told Yolanda that her mother had a stroke soon after her father was sentenced, about ten years ago, and that she and her three brothers had often gone hungry as children. As Greer drank the soda, her tears stopped and she perked up. Yolanda hesitated to ask her if she was going to be working for Tally, but Greer volunteered that she was starting on Monday.

"I'm glad," Yolanda said, relieved that she wouldn't have to feel she had to offer her a job. She couldn't afford another helper. "You'll love working for Tally. We've been good friends for years. We'd do anything for each other."

"Thanks for this," Greer said, handing back the empty can. She had emptied it so quickly, the metal was still cool. "I feel a lot better now. I'll only be part-time, but I hope I can get full-time pretty soon."

"Have you been working somewhere else?"

"I was cleaning motel rooms, but I didn't like it."

Greer left and Yolanda, still holding the empty can, thought about her last statement. How desperate was she if she had quit a job because she didn't enjoy it? She would have to wish Tally luck with this one.

* * * *

Yolanda knocked on the back door of Tally's shop after she delivered the basket to the block party. It was a perfect evening for the neighborhood night out, clear and warm, with a slight, ruffling breeze. The festivities were in full swing by the time she got there. She watched the happy revelers for only a moment before she collected her payment and left.

Tally opened the door and greeted her. Her shop, as well as Yolanda's, was closed for the night. Yolanda could smell the lingering delicious scents of the day's baking, sweet and chocolatey.

"How did it go with your new gals today?" Yolanda asked. "Are they working out?"

"I'm glad you came over. I've been dying to ask you. Where's Vi and Eden? How did it go? Did they leave?"

"They had to get back to Dallas today and work tomorrow. They came by at about noon and said good-bye in the shop. I got the impression things were tense at home and they were glad to leave."

"Poor kids. I hope your parents come around." Tally returned to scrubbing the last of the baking dishes at the sinkful of suds.

"I know. Vi has always been his favorite daughter and now Papa is barely speaking to her. I hear you hired Greer for tomorrow."

"How did you hear that?" Tally spotted a smudge of fingerprint powder behind the faucet that had been missed and swiped at it with a damp paper towel, then returned to the baking dishes.

"She was on the sidewalk in front of my shop, kind of weepy, and I had her in to try to cheer her up. We talked." Yolanda opened the refrigerator and helped herself to a Mallomar.

"I'm hiring Lily full-time. She's an excellent worker, connects well with the customers. I'm glad I found her. Molly is slow and doesn't…well, when she bakes she doesn't clean up very well. Twice today the customers told her she hadn't made the right change. I'm hoping things improve with her."

"Do you think Greer will be better?" She sat at Tally's counter and munched the gooey goody.

Tally dried the cookie sheets and stuck them into the slots in the cupboard. "It would be nice, but I don't have high hopes. Did I tell you she left without telling me on Saturday?"

"She did? Why?"

"She told Molly she felt sick, and then left without a word. She didn't look sick when she showed up today."

"Do you know her situation?"

Yolanda related what Greer had told her about her father being incarcerated and her mother having had a stroke, and the four children being hungry. Tally gave her a puzzled look.

"Get this, though," Yolanda continued. "Do you know why she left her last job?"

"No. Employers aren't allowed to tell if they've fired someone or not, so I don't bother checking references. But the thing is—"

"Y'all might want to gather some more résumés," Yolanda said. "Greer told me she left because she didn't like the job."

"Great. She shows up late, leaves without telling me, and will probably quit if I make her actually work. She also told me—"

"Do you know what's going on with the thing about Fran Abraham? I had to go to the station and answer questions this morning."

"What did they ask you? I gave them a list of everyone I could remember who was here, but I don't even know who all of them were."

"He asked me what I saw her eat and drink and who was near her. I didn't notice much, since my mind was on my parents and my sister. After my parents stormed out, I drank a lot of wine."

Tally put away the last of the utensils and hung the towel to dry. She got herself a Whoopie Pie and sat next to Yolanda. "Detective Rogers sounded like he thinks she was poisoned by something she got here. And someone told him that my dad was hanging around Fran. That's just not true! I'd like to know who said that."

"It's a mess." Yolanda rubbed her friend's shoulder, then noticed she'd gotten chocolate on her. Luckily, it was on the strap of her apron. She decided not to mention it. "Do you want to go out and do something?"

"I'm beat and I still have to go see Mom at the hospital," Tally said, her voice weary. "After that I'm going home to see my cat."

* * * *

Tally arrived at her house much later, so tired she thought of not stumbling the few extra steps to her bedroom, but sleeping on the couch instead. After she sank into the soft cushions with Nigel eagerly greeting her and demanding to be pet, Allen called again.

"Oh, Allen," she said, almost sobbing.

"What is it? What happened?"

"It's…awful." She heard highway noises. Allen must be in his truck, she thought.

"You sound like somebody died."

"She did!" Tally started blubbering.

"Who did? Your mom died?"

"No, she's in the hospital. Fran Abraham died."

"What's going on? Your mom, in the hospital? How could Fran Abraham be dead?"

Tally calmed herself with a deep breath, nuzzling her cat. "My mom has this dengue fever that she picked up on the road, in Asia, I guess."

"Is she gonna be okay?"

"I think so. But Fran… well, Fran was maybe poisoned."

"Food poisoning?"

"The detective thinks someone deliberately poisoned her. At the reception. With something that I served."

"Tally, that's crazy. You wouldn't poison anybody."

"I don't think I'm a serious suspect, but someone at the party must have done it. She keeled over right there and died very soon after, in the hospital."

"I wish I was there. I wish there was something I could do."

"I wish you were here, too, but it's helpful talking to you, Allen. I feel better than I did before you called." She heard truck horns honking.

"I better go. I have to move my rig. I'll call again to tell you when I'm coming home, as soon as I know."

Tally picked up her weary self and somehow made it to bed, snuggling with warm, rumbling Nigel for comfort.

Chapter 6

When Greer walked into the store, Tally couldn't keep the annoyance off her face. Greer came over to Tally, giving a big smile to Lily and the four customers already in the store as she passed them. Tally pulled Greer into the kitchen by her surprisingly sturdy arm.

"Do you see what time it is?"

Greer shrugged and said, still grinning, "I'm so happy to be here today."

Tally kept after her. "Tell me what time it is."

The smile finally left Greer's face. She looked at the clock on the wall. "It's a little after ten."

"It's ten minutes after ten. That makes you forty minutes late to work. On your first day."

"But you open at ten, right?"

"There's a lot to do before we open. I told you that. And I told you to be here at nine-thirty."

Greer spoke rapidly, as if that would convince Tally of something. "I know and I was totally going to do that, but my alarm didn't go off. I think something's wrong with it. I think my mom was fiddling with it."

"Your mom? You told me she's dead."

"No, I didn't mean that. She lives with me. She can't work, though."

Tally handed her a smock. "Put this on and go help Lily out there. If you work out today, you can come back to work Wednesday. I'll call you at home to wake you up."

Tally didn't miss the dirty look Greer gave her before she left the kitchen, tying the smock. No, Tally definitely wouldn't be able to keep her on. Even if she did have a sad story. Make that *several* sad stories that didn't match. Tally went into the office to call her dad's cell phone. When she'd left the hospital last night, they had sounded like they might release her mother today.

Before she could press the numbers, the desk phone rang, startling her into almost dropping her cell.

"This is Detective Rogers. If you're going to be there for a while longer, I need to come by and ask you something."

He was Jackson sometimes, when they were on good terms. During an earlier investigation that involved someone close to Tally, he was Detective Rogers. She hoped his announcement using the latter name wasn't a bad sign.

"I'm here. We're open until seven." It wasn't 10:30 yet. Why would he think she wouldn't be there? Probably just Jackson—that is, Detective Rogers—being official.

He didn't arrive until almost 11:00, leaving Tally stewing until then. She went over everything in her mind. What could he possibly want to talk to her about? She dared to think he was going to tell her that her dad was in the clear. He wanted to officially announce that to her. She made herself believe that, or at least hope so.

When he came into the shop and she saw his face at its most serious, her wishful thinking evaporated and her heart dropped an inch in her chest.

"Come into my office," she said, leading him and a uniformed policeman through the kitchen. There were only two chairs, hers and a guest chair, but the other policeman said he'd stand. He looked familiar and she took another look. It was Officer Edwards again, the large, burly man who had been at her interrogation at the station. She perched on the edge of her chair uneasily, waiting for Rogers to speak, afraid he had more evidence incriminating her father.

Rogers nodded at Officer Edwards and he set a recorder on the desk.

"Do I have your permission to record this conversation, Tally?"

"Yes, I guess so." Just so she didn't have to hear it played back. She hated the sound of her recorded voice.

"I have to get an official statement." He switched it on with a *click*. "We found something strange in the evidence we took from here, Tally."

At least he was calling her Tally and not Ms. Holt. That was good. Her spirits lifted half an inch. "Okay, what was it?"

"There was a serving platter in the trash."

"Someone threw away one of my silver platters? Why would they do that? I was using brand-new help. One of them must have done that by mistake." That wasn't such a bad thing, though. Was it? It wasn't criminal.

"We also found something even more odd," Rogers went on. "Several pastries, or whatever you call them. They looked perfectly good, uneaten, like they could have been served or sold. Do you know why they were thrown away?"

Tally shook her head. "All the food we served that didn't get eaten was thrown away. I told them to put it all in one bag so I could take it outside. I didn't notice that some was put into another trash bag, I guess. Maybe that was a mistake, too. Someone must have dumped them in with the platter. Can I have my platter back?"

"Not quite yet. It did look like those things, the platter and the food items, had been put in the wastebasket together."

Jackson's statement that Fran may have been poisoned was running through her mind. She refused to follow the thought to the place it wanted to go. "Probably just a mistake. Is that what you wanted to talk to me about?" Her fingers wanted to drum on her desk, but she held them tight so they wouldn't betray her nervousness.

"Mostly. The items were retrieved from the kitchen. Who had access to the kitchen during the event?"

"It's not locked. Anybody could come into the kitchen."

He heaved an impatient sigh. "I worded that badly, didn't I? Who did you *see* coming in or out of the kitchen?"

"The women I hired to serve. Lily, Molly, Greer. The bathroom is back here, so others may have been in the kitchen that I didn't see. Oh, my mother came back here. She was feeling sick. Maybe she shouldn't even have been at the party."

"I imagine she felt sick, since she went to the hospital, right?"

Tally gave a slight nod. Had she thrown suspicion on her mother? Surely the detective could see that she was too sick to do much. She sat on her hands to refrain from drumming her restless fingers on her desk.

"We're analyzing the pastries that were thrown away and should have the results soon. There's a rush on that and on the tox screen from Mrs. Abraham."

She knew the detective was implying that it would be a problem if the two screenings matched. "What pastries were they?" Yes, she had thrown away everything that had been on the platters and taken them to the dumpster in the alley. Why was it so suspicious that a few were put into the wastebasket in the kitchen?

"Some little round things with white filling," he said.

Whoopie Pies. Fran had eaten a few Whoopie Pies just before she collapsed. Tally felt cold inside. She told him what they were. "I don't see how Whoopie Pies could go bad. And how could anyone poison them?"

"You tell me."

"What kind of poison do you think it is?"

"A very fast-acting one."

"*If* it was the Whoopie Pies. Fran ate those just minutes before she fell down. Jackson, it can't be the Whoopie Pies. I'll never sell anything else again if people know someone got sick from them."

"Got sick and died."

Tally managed not to scream *NO NO NO* out loud, but the words reverberated inside her head.

He stood to go. "Look, I told you before. This isn't a matter of spoiled food."

The two men headed for the door.

"Are you going to tell me what the poison is when you find out?"

"That depends," Detective Rogers said and left without telling her what it depended on.

She still didn't know who had told Jackson that her father was near Fran Abraham all night. Next time she saw Jackson, she would try to get him to tell her who told him that. Who lied to him, that is.

Chapter 7

Yolanda walked toward her car in a good mood, feeling satisfied. It was hot, but beautiful. Light, fluffy clouds dotted the blue afternoon sky and a cardinal sang from one of the crape myrtles planted by the sidewalks.

The people at the real estate company loved the basket she had just delivered to them. They should, she thought. She'd gone to the trouble of buying a Monopoly game so she could use the little houses and hotels. They looked cute stuck on top of a few Mallomars from Tally's Olde Tyme Sweets. She had also fashioned miniature *For Sale* signs out of toothpicks and construction paper. She'd found a hammered tin heart online and wrote on it with markers: *Happy Tenth!* It was the tenth anniversary for the company and they were taking an extra-long lunch break at the office to celebrate the progress they'd made over the last ten years. The two champagne bottles and plastic stemware in the basket should also help with that.

A woman walked toward her, but it took her a second to recognize her as Shiny Peth. She looked uncharacteristically disheveled. She was dressed like the model she had been for a time, but her hair was mussed and she had a smear of lipstick on her cheek.

"Hi, Shiny. What are you up to?"

Shiny's large brown eyes widened. She must have been surprised to see Yolanda. "Why? What are you doing here?" Yolanda cringed at the sound of Shiny's raspy voice.

That was strange reaction, Yolanda thought. Was Shiny somewhere she shouldn't be? "I'm delivering a basket to Ranchero Real Estate. They're celebrating that they've been in business for ten years. Do you believe that? It seems like a couple of years ago when they opened up here next to the theater."

"Yeah. I remember it." Her pout looked sulky, or at least unhappy. What was wrong with her?

"Were you at the theater just now?" She had come from that direction. "I thought it would be closed, after what happened to Fran. Out of respect."

"It's closed. We had to check out a few things. Good to see you, Yolanda." She hurried on before Yolanda could start discussing Fran's horrible death with her, leaving behind a faint aroma of something alcoholic. Whiskey, Yolanda thought.

Yolanda thought about that on her drive back to Bella's Baskets. Who was "we" who were checking out "things"? Was Shiny using the empty, closed theater for a trysting place? She hoped she wasn't meeting Len there so soon after his wife died. That would be cold.

* * * *

It was noon before Tally got word of her mother getting out of the hospital. Cole called her and said he would take their parents to the hotel.

"You can take them to my house if you want to. Would that be more comfortable?"

"What? Two people sleeping on your couch? With Nigel?"

"They could have my bed, silly."

Cole had a mumbled side conversation, probably with their dad, and came back to say their parents wanted to go to the hotel. Hotels probably felt like home to them, since that's where they lived. One hotel after another. Tally wondered what they would do when they finally settled down. If they ever did. Would she have to worry about them traipsing around the globe as senior citizens? She hoped not.

"I'll get over to see them after I close, if that's okay," she said. "You'll be with them until then?"

"Most of the time. I have to pick Dorella up, since I dropped her off at work this morning."

Dorella again. What would the poor woman do when Cole left for his next artistic project?

After closing, Lily and Greer were both a big help with cleanup, Tally was glad to find. She turned off all the lights except the ones she left on for security in the front, locked up her store, and dashed home to feed Nigel.

"I'm neglecting you awfully, aren't I?" she said to the huge fur ball, talking baby talk in a high singsong. He talked back in whirs and clicks, then blinked his big eyes in appreciation, she was sure, and rubbed his head against her leg, hindering her progress in scooping food into his bowl. "I have to go see my parents, then I'll be right back. After everyone is gone and things settle down"— *whenever that will be*, she thought—"I'll spend my evenings with you."

It was nice to cuddle with Nigel, the purring machine. He was a lap snuggler in spite of his size. He could curl up to seem half as big as he was. She'd had to adjust to having him in her house, but now she didn't know what she would do if he weren't there. His arrival drew a firm line between her past and her present, and the line stretched into her future, happily.

She drove to the Sunday House Inn and Suites, where her parents were staying. As she traipsed up the stairs to their second-floor suite, she met Cole and Dorella coming down.

"Glad you're here," Cole said. "I didn't want to leave them alone, but I have to go. I'll be back soon."

He trotted down the steps before she could ask him why he had to leave. But it must have had something to do with Dorella. Everything did these last few days.

Tally opened the door to see her mother sitting up in bed and her father arranging pillows behind her.

"I'm so tired of lying down," she said. "I'll get so weak that I'll never walk again if I stay in bed too long."

"You're not going to atrophy, Nancy," her dad said. "You just have to rest and regain your strength. Do you need more to drink?"

"I'm going to float away," she said, waving him off.

"The doctor said you have to have lots of liquids, poppet."

"Fine. Later."

Tally knew that tone. It meant, "We're done talking now. What I say goes." As always, her father smiled dotingly at his wife and backed off.

"Here, have a seat." He pulled the desk chair over to the bed for Tally and went into the bathroom.

Tally gave her mother a peck on her soft cheek and sat beside her on the bed. "Are you feeling better? You look a lot better."

"It feels so good to be out of the hospital. That's no place for sick people." Her mother smiled at her own joke, then sighed, pinching her eyebrows together to wrinkle her forehead.

"What's wrong?" Tally asked.

"I need another Tylenol." She waved her hand in the direction of the desk, which was piled with bags and luggage. "There should be some in Bob's satchel."

Tally's dad had always liked to carry a bag, a sort of cross between a briefcase and a man purse. She pawed through the things heaped on the desk and found it buried beneath her mother's sweater. As she dug through the conglomeration inside it for a pill bottle, she couldn't help but notice a note with a message in large caps. She froze when she read the message:

BOB H. PAY UP OR THE COPS WILL KNOW YOUR GUILTY IN THE MURDER

She silently corrected the spelling, but wondered what this note, obviously to her father, meant. Her fingers finally closed on the plastic pill bottle and she drew it out. She wouldn't mention this note to her mother right now. The poor woman needed to concentrate on getting well if she wanted to fly to their next show on Friday.

But what should she do about the note? There were some huge implications. Wrong conclusions could be drawn. Especially by Detective Jackson Rogers.

Chapter 8

Before Tally left for work on Tuesday morning, she got a call from the detective. Dressed and heading for the front door, she saw his number with a sinking feeling of dread. What now?

"Tally, I have some bad news." Her heart sunk lower and she stumbled back into the living room. "But before I tell you, I have to know each and every person who was in your kitchen between the time the Whoopie Pies were made and when they were served."

"Fran was poisoned with my Whoopie Pies?" She sank onto the couch, glad she'd been standing next to it. She was also glad she was home and not at her shop. She had to contain this news somehow. She couldn't possibly let any customers hear that she might have served poison to anyone.

"I'm asking you to give me all the names you can. Then I'll check with each of them. We have to know about everyone."

"But that means Fran died of my Whoopie Pies. That's what you're saying, isn't it?" Tally couldn't keep the sob from her voice. Nigel rubbed against her right leg, gazing up at her with a wide-eyed look of sympathy, as she unconsciously petted him. "What will I do? Can you not tell anyone about it? Until you find out what happened."

She could hear Detective Rogers take a breath and imagined him counting to ten. "I'm not telling anyone. I'm even not telling you, actually."

That was true. He hadn't said it—she had. "I'll call you back and give you a list again."

She broke the connection before she became unable to speak. Her fist in her mouth, she muffled her sobs as much as she could, and her crying jag was over in a few minutes. Nigel jumped into her lap. She wondered if he actually sensed her distress, like a person would. His weight in her lap was comforting. He made his strange little chirping noises, which made her smile.

Feeling calmer and strangely cleansed after her cry, she listed the names on a piece of paper. Nigel gazed at them with a wise expression. They were the same ones she already had told the detective: Lily, Molly, Greer, her mother going to the bathroom. The gathering that night hadn't lasted as long as it could have, even as long as she'd planned for, what with her mother getting sick and with Fran...collapsing. It was probable that some others had used the restroom, too, but she hadn't kept tabs on everyone. She'd been busy trying to keep up with her help, the food and drinks, and the drama in the Bella family.

* * * *

Something had been bothering Yolanda ever since she remembered about it two days ago, on Sunday morning, the day after Fran's murder. She had to tell someone about it. She glanced at the clock in her shop. Both she and Tally opened at 10:00 and it was now 9:30. Knowing Tally would be there, she went through the alley to her back door.

"Knock, knock," she called as she came into the kitchen.

Tally was shoving a batch of something, maybe Twinkies, into the oven. She thought Lily must have been in the front room.

"Whatcha got?" Tally's face had a pinched look.

"Is everything okay?" Yolanda said. "Something's worrying y'all." Yolanda helped herself to a half a cup from the kitchen coffee urn and pulled out a stool to perch on.

Tally glanced in the direction of the front of the store. "I'll tell you later. I don't want to talk about it here."

"Something's worrying me, too, and I have to tell someone before I burst."

Tally starting wiping down her counter. That woman was always working. She didn't have any lazy bones, Yolanda thought.

"Shoot," Tally said, scrubbing at a stubborn spot.

"I have two somethings, but I'll start with the good one."

"You're smiling. Something to do with Kevin?"

"Is it that obvious? Yes, we had dinner last night and...well, it went very well. He's growing on me, more and more every day."

"I think it's probably mutual."

"I hope so." Yolanda sipped her coffee before launching into the other point. "Here's the other something. Ionia Goldenberger came into Bella's

Baskets about a week ago, maybe longer, and she said something that's been bothering me. It's about…the murder."

Tally stopped working and stood very still. "But this was way before…"

Yolanda nodded. "She asked if I'd heard the rumors about Fran. I didn't know what she was talking about, so she told me. She said there were rumors that Fran was using material she hadn't paid for."

"What do you mean?"

"The theater has to rent the scripts from places that give them licenses to use them. You're supposed to get enough copies for everyone and pay for them. Ionia accused Fran of not renting enough and making her own copies. Not paying for the copies you need is dishonest and, Ionia said, could get Fran fired as director of the theater. I don't know if it's illegal or not, but it's against the agreement, she said. That is, she told me she was repeating the rumors she had heard."

"Interesting. She accused my mother of stealing material from *her*. Mom's stuff is all original these days. She and Dad write their songs. So Fran doesn't write her own material?"

"Ionia told me she's done a few, but mostly puts on plays that everyone has heard of. Not her originals." Yolanda paused to take another sip of coffee. "When Fran was murdered, I remembered what Ionia told me about the rumors."

"What does all that have to do with her death?"

"Not that. It's the rest of what Ionia said. After she told me all of this, she admitted she felt bad—she had started the rumors herself and they weren't true at all."

"That's awful! Why did she do that?"

"Ionia thought she should have Fran's job. She wanted to, she said, 'Get Fran out of the way.'"

"Get her out of the way? There's another method of doing that, besides getting her fired, right? Like…murdering her? Are you going to tell this to the police?"

"I'm not sure. Do you think I should?"

"Yes, you should! They think my dad killed her!"

"Oh, no, Tally!" Yolanda caught her friend's hand and held it a moment. It trembled slightly.

Lily came into the kitchen. "Time to open?"

* * * *

After Yolanda left, Tally started shaking all over. She retreated to the bathroom to think about what she had just learned. If there was a chance Ionia had killed Fran, her dad was off the hook. She hoped Yolanda would go to the police very soon. She had urged her to do that. Tears of relief streamed down her face. After a minute or two, she emerged from the bathroom, after making sure her eyes weren't red and her face wasn't tearstained, to find her father in the kitchen.

"What are you doing here?" She wasn't upset to see him there, just puzzled.

"I talked to your detective this morning. He gave me a heads-up on something and I want to ask you to help me watch out for someone."

"He talked to you about Fran?" The detective had been busy on the phone today.

"No, this is nothing to do with her death. It's about someone who's in prison. Someone I know."

Her father knew a person who was in prison? That was surprising.

He continued. "The man, Wendell Samson, is eligible for parole. Rogers says he may be released soon. If you see him around town, I want you to let me know." He handed her a picture torn from a newspaper, the paper old and yellowed. The man pictured wore a coarse-looking shirt with wide stripes and held a number in front of him. He was obviously going to prison. The picture was black-and-white, but she could tell his too-long hair was darkish. He had a narrow, clean-shaven face and his hostile eyes squinted at the camera.

Tally looked at the picture, then at her father. "Who is he to you? How do you know him?"

"We had a run-in many years ago. It's possible he holds me responsible for some things."

"He's from Fredericksburg?"

Bob Holt nodded.

"Do you want to talk to him if I see him?"

"No! I mean—no, I don't. I just want to know if he's in town." He held his hand out for her to return the picture.

"How old is this picture?"

"I told you, it was a long time ago."

"But it's old, right? I'm not sure I'll know it's him if I see him. He could look a lot different."

"Yes, he could. But if someone like him comes around asking about me, don't tell him anything. Don't tell him I'm in town. Just let me know, okay, sweetheart?"

He hugged her and she gave him her assurances that she would. She gave him some treats for him and her mom.

She watched him walk out the door, left with an uneasy feeling.

Mrs. Gerg walked in as Tally's dad was leaving. A string of plastic beads dangled from her fingers.

"Oh, look, the colors are perfect," she said, holding the beads up to Tally's apron. "I knew they would be, the moment I saw them."

Tally was reluctant to accept the cheap necklace, but Mrs. Gerg meant well, she knew. It took very little to make her landlady happy. All she had to do was accept her gifts. And pay her rent on time. Mrs. Gerg was a short, sturdy woman with thin, curly hair, who usually wore a pair of nearly worn-out shoes, run over at the heels. Tally wished she would find shoes for herself at the garage sales she loved to frequent, instead of buying useless gifts for her tenant. Although, maybe those awful-looking shoes were comfortable.

Tally slipped the beads over her head. The deep purple did look nice with her smock, which was a soft lilac color. Mrs. Gerg bought one Clark Bar and left, a smile on her cherubic face.

That night after the shop closed, she went to the hotel to see her parents, first stopping in to feed Nigel, scoop out the litter box, and sit with him in her lap for a few calming moments. It surprised her that tending to the litter box was turning out to be a less onerous task than she'd thought it would be. The large, lovable cat always stood by and kept a close watch while she invaded what he probably thought of as his personal territory. She knew that she didn't like people poking around in her bathroom. They could use it, but she had a horror of strangers looking into her medicine cabinets and her toiletries. It wasn't that she had anything to hide—she just considered those things personal. Maybe Nigel felt the same way.

After a brief, but effective, attitude adjustment brought about by purring and head rubbing, Tally drove to the Sunday House Inn. She paused outside the door when she heard her parents' raised voices. They sounded distressed. Her stomach clenched. A good loud knock, she hoped, would warn them. She banged on the door.

Her father answered the door. He bent so his face was close to hers and whispered that he didn't want her to say anything about what he'd told her this morning and she gave him a nod, still puzzled about that, and feeling uneasy about her father holding secrets from his past.

She peeked around him to see that her mother was crying. "Are you feeling worse?" Tally asked, distressed.

"No, she's feeling a lot better," Tally's father answered.

Tally scowled at him for answering the question. "I asked Mom."

Nancy Holt was sitting on the side of the unmade bed. She'd obviously been in it for at least part of the day. Tally sat beside her.

"What's wrong? Are you in pain?"

"No, she's not in pain." Again, Bob Holt answered for his wife.

"I'm not asking you, Dad!" Tally gave him a pointed, exasperated look. "Mom?" Tally took her mother's hand and gently massaged the back of it. She realized, as she hadn't before, that her mother was getting older. The veins in her hand stood out and her skin was more wrinkled than Tally remembered. When had she last taken a good look at her? She did so now and saw an attractive, thin woman who seemed afraid.

"The detective," Nancy finally said, "wants to talk to me."

"Well, sure," Tally said. "He wants to talk to everyone."

"No, he suspects me." Nancy reached for a tissue on the bedside table and dabbed at her eyes. Her face looked naked without the full complement of makeup she usually wore.

"I'm sure he doesn't. He's talking to every—"

"He does! He has to. Everyone heard me arguing with Fran, threatening her."

"You didn't threaten to kill her!"

"I threatened to ruin her in this town. I think those were my exact words."

Bob spoke. "Don't you think that's a leap? From ruining a reputation to killing a person?"

"That's the best way to get rid of horrible people," Nancy said. "People who lie about you."

Tally thought her mother was being hysterical, but she wasn't going to tell her that. She was still sick. Maybe that's why she was overreacting. On the other hand, Tally thought that the dustup between the women might give her father a good motive in the eyes of the law. He adored his wife. Tally had seen him warn people off when they were not treating her well. She had even seen him even attack a man once.

It was a few years ago, when Tally and Cole were still touring with them, doing their brother-sister act on stage. They tap-danced, rudimentary steps—Tally never did manage to master the art, though Cole wasn't bad, and sang a duet—"You Are My Sunshine" with a simple two-part harmony in old-fashioned matching costumes, resembling the kids from *Our Gang.* At one show that stuck in Tally's mind, a man in the front row booed and called out insults during their act. Tally and Cole both left the stage in tears.

"That man said I was stupid," Tally wailed. "And ugly."

Cole was sniffling, too, though not complaining as much as his sister.

Her mother held her small daughter and stroked her head, done up in tight curls at the time, and Tally was soon soothed. Her father patted Cole's shoulder and told them to ignore the heckler, that there would be others at other shows and that they had to get used to it. And anyway, he was drunk, their dad said. She wondered if that was what their mother would call a "lame excuse." Tally couldn't remember seeing anyone as nasty as that before, and they'd been touring for a long time.

Anyway, the next piece that night was a dramatic reading from a scene in Tennessee Williams's *Cat on a Hot Tin Roof.* Their mother dressed in a simple white slip, played Maggie, and their father wore a bathrobe to play Brick, using a cane to hobble around the stage. Tally always thought they did a magnificent job, playing the scene vividly without any props or background. They talked about the family and their troubles and the scene ended with Nancy, as Maggie, crying that she was living with someone who didn't love her and it had turned her into a cat on a hot tin roof. The piece usually brought thunderous applause, but this time the audience could barely hear the lines over the clamor of the drunken man, telling them to put their clothes on and grow up, and get over...something...Tally forgot what. He was especially vicious about Nancy/Maggie, yelling out that no wonder Brick didn't love her, she was so ugly.

Tally and Cole were, as always, watching from the wings. They were shocked when their dad jumped off the stage, balled up his fists, and started punching the drunk heckler.

From then on, Tally knew that her dad's breaking point was her mother. He wouldn't tolerate anyone insulting her.

And Fran had certainly insulted her.

Chapter 9

Tally shook her head to clear the bad childhood memory from her mind and returned to Tuesday evening in her parents' room at the Sunday House Inn and Suites.

"Did you like the things I sent you?" she asked her mom.

"Things you sent me? Oh, you mean the Clark Bars and fudge? Yes, I ate some." Nancy turned her head and looked straight at her daughter, her tears and trembling stopped for now. "You know, you're very good at this. Those things you make are delicious."

"Well...thanks, Mom." Tally broke out beaming. Maybe her parents were beginning to accept her career choice. She often thought they never would. They seemed to want her and her brother to remain in the past, on the stage with them.

"Yes, I did like them. In fact, I didn't finish that second Clark Bar. Is it still here, Bob?"

Tally's dad nodded and produced it from a dresser drawer, half-eaten and wrapped in a napkin. The chocolate fragrance made Nancy Holt's face light up.

"I think I'd like to finish it now," she said, reaching for it.

"Chocolate always makes me feel better," Tally said, approving of her mother's actions. Maybe now she would stop crying about and dwelling upon her upcoming interview with the detective. She wanted to ask her mother when she was going to the police station, but didn't want to bring up the subject again.

As she left, about half an hour later, she pulled her father halfway out the door and asked him.

"Tomorrow morning," he said. "She's supposed to be there at ten."

Ten o'clock was when her shop opened. She wished it were earlier so she could go with them. "Tell me what happens as soon as you can, okay?" If she didn't have brand-new employees, she could maybe have entrusted the shop to them.

"Love you, punkin pie." He leaned down and kissed her on the forehead, just as he had always done when she was a child, about to go onto the stage.

She left before he could see her tears.

* * * *

The next morning, Tally's mind was on her parents, on her father's possible shady past—tied up with a convicted criminal—and on her mother's interview at the police station as she flipped her *Open* sign and made sure the door was unlocked. She decided to carry her cell phone in the pocket of her smock and even turned the volume up all the way to the loud end of the bar, something she didn't usually do while working. If her father called, she didn't want to miss it.

Lily called early to say she had to be at the police station for questioning. When she got in, soon after opening, Tally asked her how it went.

"Okay. They just asked me where I was and what I was doing at the reception. They don't think I killed Fran. At least, I hope they don't. They let me go. That's good, isn't it?"

"Yes." Tally had to grin. "That's very good. Did you see my parents there? They were supposed to go in at ten."

"No, they weren't there when I left."

Tally decided she would wait for one of them to call her. She had gotten some of the merchandise out, but hadn't finished. Lily got right to work and helped get the rest of the treats from the refrigerator and arranged them in the display case. At 10:45, Greer still hadn't shown up. Tally decided she was fresh out of patience and phoned Molly to come in. Molly hemmed and hawed a bit, but said she could get there by noon.

Greer showed up as soon as Tally finished the call to Molly. A cloud of pungent, fruity smoke accompanied her. Tally swatted the sweet, rotten odor away from her own face and motioned for Greer to come into the kitchen.

"Have a seat," Tally said, in case Greer would need to be sitting to get the news she was about to deliver.

The young woman climbed onto the stool at the work counter, giving Tally a smile. "I can explain why I'm late."

"You don't need to," Tally said, feeling like the Wicked Witch of the West. She looked Greer in the eye, then looked away. "I won't need you here after all. I can't use someone who isn't dependable."

Greer's mouth gaped wide open for several seconds, then she recovered herself. "I'm dependable! I told you I can explain!"

"Please keep your voice down. There are customers in the store."

"I guess Yolanda was wrong. She told me you are one of her best friends and that you are a good person." Greer hopped off the stool and stood inches from Tally. Her breath smelled rank from whatever she had been smoking just before she came in. "I can do this job. Don't fire me or…"

"Or?" Tally asked, backing away. "Do you know how bad you smell? You can't work here selling things to eat with that cloud of cigarette smoke."

"It's not cigarettes. It's e-cigarettes. They don't smell." She shoved her face in Tally's, disproving her words.

"Greer, I'm not going to quibble. I hired you on probation and it didn't work out."

They stood toe to toe for a moment. Tally was determined not to back away again. Greer finally gave in, spun, and stomped out through the customers. Tally watched her go, relieved that she didn't make a scene in the salesroom.

Greer didn't disappear right away, though. After phoning or texting someone, she hung around in front of the store for five or ten minutes. Then a man drove up in an old green beat-up pickup. Greer climbed in as Tally ducked to try to see what he looked like, but only got the impression of a silhouette—a man wearing a gimme cap.

Soon after that, she realized she should pay Greer for the few hours she had worked. She'd paid everyone for the reception, but not yet for any of their work afterward in the shop.

Molly, as promised, came in at noon and got to work beside Lily. The customers were coming in waves. First a crowd, then one or two by themselves, then another crowd.

Tally kept an eye on both of her new hires. She considered they were on probation, also, but she'd decided to keep Lily a long time ago. Her mind wasn't made up about Molly yet. At one point Tally sent her to the kitchen to get more wares. The fudge was selling well today and getting low. When Molly didn't return, Tally went looking for her. She had dumped a batch of Truffle Fudge on the kitchen floor and was trying to put the pieces back on one of the trays used to bring things to the front.

"Molly, what are you doing?"

She looked up from where she knelt, scooping up the pieces. "They won't be able to tell. It didn't get smushed."

"No! We can't sell those. What are you thinking? You go out front. I'll get something to fill the empty space."

Molly gave her boss an exasperated look as she passed her. Tally didn't appreciate that one bit.

She busied herself selecting some more goodies and arranging the case in the front, keeping her eye on Molly.

She had another eye on the clock. It was well after noon. Why hadn't she heard from her father about the questioning at ten o'clock? They had to have been at the police station for hours. She tried calling him twice, but he didn't answer. She wasn't going to call her mother. If she wasn't in a better state of mind than she had been last night, Tally wouldn't be able to speak to her on the phone. She would want to dash over to her, wherever she was.

A fleeting image of her mother behind bars flitted through her mind and she shooed it out and looked around the shop.

Lily was ringing up a nice, big sale. Molly was nearby with a potential buyer who was looking at the Mallomars. Molly leaned in close to the customer and probably thought she was speaking more quietly than she was.

Tally was horrified when she heard Molly tell the man that she didn't think the Mallomars were very good. "The recipe doesn't use enough chocolate," she whispered. "It should be thicker."

The man gave her a surprised look.

"And I don't know why they cost this much. The ingredients are pretty cheap."

He frowned at Molly and walked out of the store.

Tally closed the short distance between them in two seconds. "You need to straighten up," Tally said. "That was awful. You should know better than that."

Molly looked just as amazed as Greer had. "Why? What did I do? I've been selling things to people. I can't help it if every single person doesn't buy stuff."

"You don't use the word 'cheap' to describe products you're trying to sell. You don't tell the customer that our candies don't taste very good. And you don't sell dirty fudge that you've dropped on the floor."

Tally could read the guilt on her face, knowing she'd been overheard.

She couldn't get rid of both of them, Greer *and* Molly. That would leave her too shorthanded. She would have to give Molly another chance. She couldn't run the shop with only her and Lily and didn't have time to look for someone else.

Tally told Molly to come back the next day. "Just hang your smock on the hook and please leave out the back."

Molly threw her smock in the direction of the hook, but did return and pick it up after it landed on the floor. She didn't look back as she left.

Tally felt a queasiness overcome her insides and told Lily she needed to go to her office for a minute.

"Don't take too long. We'll probably get busy as soon as you leave," Lily said. Tally knew she was right.

Tally plopped into her desk chair, closed her eyes, and did some deep breathing to calm her jangled nerves. To her utter surprise, it worked.

When she opened her eyes, her hands were steady and she realized she was relieved to be rid of both Molly and Greer for the afternoon. While she was at her desk, she might as well see if she could quickly figure out how much she owed all of them and get checks ready to mail. She had been keeping records, so it was a matter of a couple of minutes to figure the tax and make out the checks. Then she pulled their files to get the addresses.

All the files had their applications and the ID copies she had made. She pulled the sheets out with the photocopies of their driver's licenses. After she wrote Greer's address on an envelope, she glanced again at her application sheet.

Her phone picked that moment to go off. It was Allen. Tally quickly answered the call. "Yeah? Allen?"

"Yes, I'm Allen. You sound—"

"I'm in the middle of something. I can't talk right now. I'll call you later."

She put her phone down and returned to the papers. Something didn't look right. Tally set the sheets side by side. The picture on Molly's driver's license was clear, as was Lily's, but the one on Greer's was blurry. She put Molly's and Greer's sheets on top of the other, turned on her bright desk lamp, and held them up to it. The fonts were different.

Tally fell back into her chair. One of them was fake. She could hear people coming in, ringing the door chime, and more than a few voices in the salesroom. Maybe Yolanda or Cole could look at these and tell what was what. She shoved everything into her middle drawer, locked it, and hurried to help Lily.

* * * *

At last, it was time to close. Tally flipped the sign, leaned on the door, then sank against it all the way to the floor.

"Tally?" Lily, removing trays of candies and sweets to put into the refrigerator, shot her a look of concern.

"It was a hard day, don't you think? Well, maybe harder for me. I feel awful that I had to fire Greer."

"I'll tell you, I'm glad you did. Neither one of those women is easy to work with."

"Thank you, Lily. That makes me feel a little better. I want to give Molly another chance, though. I think she could work out, after I've laid down the law today." She shoved herself off the door and went to help Lily close up.

As she was finishing the wipe down in the kitchen, Tally knocked two baking pans onto the floor. They had been washed and were drying on the countertop.

The clatter made both women jump. Lily picked them up and plunged them into the sink to rewash.

Tally thanked her. "I'm so clumsy today."

"You're right. You dropped that roll of quarters all over the floor earlier." Tally had been refilling the till and had been all thumbs.

"You'll be better tomorrow," Lily said, reassuring her.

"I'm not sure I will be." Tally stopped what she was doing to face Lily. "I probably should tell you this. Both of my parents are, as near as I can tell, prime suspects for the murder of Fran."

"What? That's crazy. They don't even live here."

"They've all three known each other for a long time. All four, counting Fran's husband."

"But how about the people working in the theater now? They are with her every day. I've worked with her, too, so I know. Lots of them are happy to have her out of the way."

Tally remembered that Lily was a dancer at the theater when they did an occasional musical. "What do you know about them? The theater people?"

"Plenty. And I've told the detective, too."

"You have?" If Lily had mentioned other people, why was Jackson picking on her parents? "Who are they? Which ones?"

"At least a couple. For instance, Ionia. She's been on the outs with Fran for the last few years. I can't blame her for feeling that she should be the director. I'd like her to be the director, too. Probably most people would. She's easy to work with. But Ionia told me—and I know she's told other people—that Fran says she writes her songs, when everyone knows she doesn't. Ionia says Fran steals other people's music and cheats the script rental places. I think that's awful. And Shiny Peth? She could have done it."

"Yes, I noticed at the reception the way she hung on Lennie. Why would she kill Fran, though? She seemed to be monopolizing Fran's husband just fine while Fran was alive."

"She really hated Fran after she was fired and told never to come back. Shiny loves the stage. I've even heard her say she wished Fran were dead."

"And you told all of that to the detective?"

"He wrote it down while I was telling him. Maybe he'll quit bothering your parents once he gets all his interviews done."

Tally thought he had done a lot of interviews already. But her parents were still on the hook.

Chapter 10

Nigel snuggled in Tally's lap, his purr a noisy rumble.

"Life is simple for you, isn't, it?" she crooned, stroking his silky fur, which turned his volume up even higher. He gave her a skeptical look. Maybe, from his standpoint, his life wasn't any easier than hers. When she'd gotten home just now, after dropping the checks in the mail, she found that he had put all his toys under the couch and was stretching a paw, futilely, trying to retrieve them. He was dependent on her for food, a clean litter box, toy retrieval, and…well, everything.

"Okay, maybe not simple. But you don't have to deal with a tunnel-visioned homicide detective and worrisome employees and the headaches of running a business."

He must have agreed, because he rested his chin on his huge paws and closed his eyes, bringing the purr volume down to a dull roar.

Second thoughts plagued her. Should she have fired Greer? Could she have tried harder to educate her? Could she continue to employ Molly? She had to teach her how to deal with customers and not betray her employer. Also, was she extra-touchy today because she was so worried about her parents?

Thoughts of her parents drove her up from the couch to try to find out how they were doing. She hadn't heard from them all day. Nigel protested when she dumped him onto the floor, but she refreshed his kibble and he forgave her. Or so she imagined as she drove to the hotel.

She listened for a moment when she got there before she rapped on their door. She didn't hear raised voices today. Or her mother crying. That was a good sign.

When her father opened the door, though, he didn't look good. His face was pale, stunned.

"What's happening, Dad? Are you all right?"

"No, he's not all right," her mother piped up from the reading chair. "The detective had him in again this afternoon."

"Again?"

"He said there are three sets of fingerprints on the platter that held the poisoned food."

"Mine and Greer's. Who else's?" Tally said.

"Mine," her father said.

Tally took his hand and guided him to the bed. He seemed dazed, like he might fall over any moment.

"He told you that?" Tally asked, wondering why the detective would do that. To make her father confess, because then he would "know" that the police were onto him? One of those ploys, those police tricks to get people to talk?

Her father stared at the floor, his face slack and his eyes dull and hopeless. "He changed the way he was speaking. He sounded very tough, I thought. He said, and this is a quote: 'We know you handled that platter. We know your fingerprints are all over it.' Then he stared at me so hard I thought he was going to drill through my eyeballs to the back of my head."

"What did you do, Dad?" It did sound like Jackson wanted her father to confess, right there.

"I sat there like a mounted butterfly with a pin through my middle."

"Then what?" Indignation was swelling inside Tally. How dare he browbeat her father that way?

"Nothing. I couldn't think of anything to say for a couple of minutes. Then I said I may have touched it, but I don't remember."

"Bob," Tally's mother said. "I think I saw that young woman ask you to hold it."

Bob Holt's eyes widened as he spun toward his wife. "That's right, she did. I'd forgotten. She said to hold it while she did something. Retied her apron or something."

"Oh dear," Tally said. Another thought came to her. Not a good one. "Does the detective also know how much you like cooking, baking things, working in the kitchen?"

He shook his head. "But I wasn't in your kitchen that day."

"Dad, you were there the night before," Tally said.

He nodded. "Yes, we did see the kitchen when we came in."

She knew his fingerprints were in the room. She pictured him leaning against her counter, his hand resting on the surface. Had his prints been wiped off? Thoroughly wiped off?

"Mom," she said. "Who was it that asked him to hold the platter?"

"One of your workers." Nancy Holt waved a graceful hand through the air. "I don't really remember which one."

Her father didn't, either. It was one of the three, that's all Tally knew.

She turned to her mother. "What happened this morning, Mom? How did your interview go?"

Her mother looked at the wall. "It was okay. I don't want to talk about it."

After she left her parents, she called Yolanda from her car before she started for home. She had to talk to someone.

* * * *

Yolanda was so worried about how Tally sounded on the phone, she told her to come over right away. When she opened her door to her, Tally looked even worse than she had sounded—frantic, panicked.

"Tally, what's the matter?"

Yolanda led her to the brocade couch that took up a large part of her small living room.

"Do y'all need something to drink? I have a bottle of wine Kevin gave me the other day."

Tally's shoulders fell. "I'd better not start drinking anything alcoholic, the way I feel right now. I might not stop."

"I'll just get some iced tea."

Yolanda was back in a minute and handed Tally a cold glass. Tally gulped half of it.

"I guess I'm thirsty." She looked up at Yolanda. "There's a good case against my dad."

"Case? What case?"

"For killing Fran."

Yolanda, stunned, slowly wilted onto the couch next to Tally. "Killing Fran? Who says?"

"No one said it, but I can tell by what Dad has told me. He's been questioned more than once and today Jackson told him his prints are on the platter where the poisoned Whoopie Pies were."

"So what? Lots of people touched all the platters. We were eating, for gosh sakes. Tell your dad that. Or tell Jackson. Why is that a big deal?"

"It's the way Jackson was saying it. That's what Dad said. Like accusing him."

"There's no way your dad killed anyone. Even Fran Abraham." Yolanda was glad to see that her last remark brought a slight grin to Tally's sad face. "He doesn't have to worry if that's all the evidence there is."

Tally sat silent another moment, took two sips, then seemed to fold her shoulders in even more, to shrink up small. "I know something that the police don't know. That they probably should know. I'm afraid to ask my dad about it."

It was Yolanda's turn for stunned silence. Tally had evidence against her own father? Was it possible, remotely possible, that Bob Holt had poisoned Fran Abraham? Yolanda took Tally's almost-empty glass. Tally looked ready to drop it.

"I was digging in my dad's bag for some pain pills for Mom and found a piece of paper with a threat written on it. It looked like a blackmail note."

"Your dad hasn't done anything a person could blackmail him for." Yolanda was certain of that. "What did it say? Do you remember?"

"I can't forget it. I keep picturing it over and over in my head." Tally drummed her fingers on the arm of the couch. "It says, 'Bob H. Pay up or the cops will know you're guilty in the murder.' Except that the word *you're* was misspelled."

"When did you find that?"

"Right after Mom got out of the hospital."

"What did your dad say about it?"

Tears tumbled from Tally's eyes. "That's just it. He hasn't said a thing. Wouldn't he say something? Wouldn't he be surprised? I mean, if he didn't know what it meant?"

"I don't follow," Yolanda said. "How would he know what that meant?"

"If he were actually guilty in the murder, like it said. Then he'd know what it meant."

"I…guess you're right. But… But how? Tally, that can't be."

"I know," Tally wailed and started sobbing. "It can't be."

After her friend was cried out and finally became calm enough to drive home, Yolanda walked her to her little blue Chevy and watched her drive away, her taillights slowly receding, until they turned into her own driveway, three blocks down. Yolanda returned to her own front door, her head down, pondering the woes of the world. And specifically, those of her and Tally.

The worst of her own problems right now was the family tension due to her sister coming out to their parents. Maybe it hadn't been a good idea to do it in public, at the reception, after all. When Papa had met Violetta's friend, Eden, he had stormed out, their mother trailing along in his wake and left the two stunned women staring after them in disbelief.

Yolanda and Violetta had discussed options after that and finally decided that they should all show up to dinner that evening, as planned.

"What's the worst thing that can happen?" Violetta had said. "It couldn't be worse than the public snubbing they gave us already today."

So all three young women had gone to dinner. Yolanda knew her mama had worked for hours preparing Vi's favorite foods. She knew her mother. The woman wouldn't want all that food to go to waste. Yolanda even thought she would have been welcoming to her daughter's friend if it weren't for her husband's attitude.

Mrs. Bella showed them in and they went right to the table instead of the usual predinner relaxation ritual, which was having drinks and maybe some cheese and crackers, and casual chat. At the table, it was right to the business of eating. The meal was tense, Mrs. Bella making conversation with the young women and—her mistake—trying to draw her husband into their discussions. His answers were either silence or grunts, never raising his head or ceasing from shoveling the food into his mouth as fast as possible, so he could leave the table when everyone else was half through eating.

Luckily, none of them had planned on staying overnight that night. They hurried through dessert without the man of the house. Then, after an interval barely long enough to be polite, they departed, Yolanda to her own tiny Sunday House, and Vi and Eden to a rented room at a B and B. Vi told her sister they would drive back to Dallas that night. They had planned on staying through Sunday, but what was the point? The meeting of the parents had gone so badly, none of them wanted to prolong it.

Since then, Yolanda had phoned her sister a couple of times. Neither had spoken to their parents.

"Are y'all planning on meeting Eden's parents, Vi?" Yolanda had asked her during one of the calls.

"We have to sooner or later."

"Does she know what their reaction will be?"

"Not really. They already know she's not straight. She had a girlfriend two years ago for a short time and they were okay with that."

"Oh, good. So it won't be a problem that you're together. Do you know how they'll feel about you?"

"It might be a problem. If they find out our mother is Hispanic, they won't like that."

Yolanda had let out a discouraged breath. Another problem parent. Just what they didn't need. "I'm sorry you two are having such problems. We're both fairly light-skinned. Maybe you shouldn't tell them."

"Then what would happen when the two sets of parents meet someday?"

"If they meet," Yolanda had said. But she knew her sister was right. They had to tell them sooner, not later.

Chapter 11

Tally sat petting the rumbling Nigel in her dark living room. She was feeling nearly overwhelmed by her worries tonight. There was also a nagging regret on her mind for not having asked Yolanda how her sister was. Tally knew, from the confrontation at the reception, of course, that the elder Bellas were not happy about their daughter's new romance. She didn't even know if they had spoken since then, or if things had smoothed over at all. Next time she saw Yolanda she would definitely bring up the subject.

Her biggest worry eclipsed that regret, though. That was the blackmail note. She had to admit that's what it obviously was. And it was addressed to her father. She had tried to think her way out of the obvious, but she couldn't. How would a missive addressed to another Bob H. end up in her father's satchel? It wouldn't. It was meant for him. She pictured her accidental find again. The paper was well-creased and didn't look new, though. Wouldn't something mentioning the very recent murder look newer?

Should she ask her dad about it? That wasn't something she wanted to do. Not at all. Maybe she could ask her mother? If it was a secret, though, would her mother know what it was about? Blackmail notes, notes asking people to pay up, were always about secrets, weren't they? Otherwise, the threat to expose whatever it was wouldn't be a threat.

"I'm so confused," she said to Nigel.

He blinked wisely, but had no solutions.

"About what?"

Her brother's voice startled her. She hadn't heard him come in. It was well after eleven o'clock and she'd assumed he wasn't staying at her place that night. She would tell Cole. He should know and he might have an idea of what to do.

"Sis, are you okay? You're sitting in the dark again."

Her brother knew that when she did that, she wasn't in the best of moods.

"Sit down," she said. "I have a couple of things to ask you."

Cole snatched a beer from the kitchen and returned to the living room, switching on a table lamp as he sat on the couch. When she told Cole where she'd found the note and quoted it to him, he fell silent.

At last he spoke. "You and I know Dad didn't kill that woman."

"The paper looked a little yellow and it had been folded many, many times."

"You're thinking there was a murder before this and he was involved in that?"

They stared into each other's eyes, fright zinging between them.

"I don't want to ask Dad about this," Tally said.

"No, no, you shouldn't. Not right now, when there's this other thing hanging over his head. It's something from long ago. Leave it there for him." Cole took a swig from the beer can. "How about asking Mom about it?"

"Could she handle it better? She's still sick with that dengue fever."

"Mom usually handles a crisis better than Dad, don't you think?" Cole asked.

Tally had to admit that their mother had come through, calmly and competently, when they'd had booking problems on the road. Even now, for instance, she didn't seem to be as worried about her illness as their father was. Even though she was getting the proper treatment and everyone had been assured she would recover, their dad hovered and fussed no end.

"If I talk to her, it'll be in the morning," Tally decided.

"Are you going to do that?"

They reached no conclusion, but Tally remembered something else she wanted to talk to Cole about.

"I have something at the office I'd like you to look at tomorrow. I wish I'd brought them home so you could see them now."

"See what?" He finished off the beer and crushed the can with a crinkling sound.

"I think one of my hires gave me a fake driver's license."

Cole raised his eyebrows and gave her a wary look. "And you think I know what fake driver's licenses look like?"

"Oh, come on. I know you had one in high school."

"Well, yeah, I did, but they probably make them differently now. They didn't have those fancy hidden things on them then. Holograms, or whatever they are. They were easier to fake."

When she glared at him, he smiled, his deep dimples emerging on his handsome face. "Okay, big sister, I'll look at them. I can come by tomorrow."

"Call first to see if I'm slammed at the store."

Tally got up to sleep in her bed so Cole could have the couch. The cat wanted to sleep with Cole that night. Her brother was, after all, Nigel's former owner.

Tally hadn't settled any of her dilemmas. She wondered if she ever could. She tossed for over an hour before sleep came.

* * * *

Tally's sleep was brief, as her night was shortened on both ends. After she went to bed past midnight, well after her usual time, she was awakened early by a phone call.

"Uh, yes?" she mumbled through her sleep. The number was from the police station, she was pretty sure. "Who is this?"

"Tally, this is Jackson."

Now she was wide awake. She squinted at her alarm clock. 3:30. "Jackson? What—what is it? What's wrong?"

"I wanted to be the one to tell you. Your father has been arrested."

"Arrested? For what?" She was yelling, she knew. "You can't arrest him."

Cole was already at her bedroom door, his face puckered with worry. *Dad?* he mouthed. Tally nodded and Cole dropped beside her onto the bed.

"You arrested him in the middle of the night?" she said, her voice turned down a notch in volume.

Nigel padded into the bedroom and joined them on the bed. He looked worried, too.

"I know," Jackson said. "But I didn't want you to hear it from someone else."

"Can I talk to him?" she asked.

When he said she could not, she asked where her mother was. She pictured her poor mom, dizzy and sick, sitting at the police station in her bathrobe.

"She's back at the hotel. She was here for a while, but one of the officers drove her back to the hotel just now."

After Tally hung up, her tears came. She and Cole hugged for a few minutes, then Tally asked him if he thought they should call their mom.

"No," Cole said. "I think we should go over there."

"You're right." Tally pulled her jeans on. "She can't be asleep with this going on. Turn around." She tugged her nightgown off and slipped into a bra and tee. Cole was dressed by the time she got her shoes on and they headed over to the Sunday House Inn and Suites in his rented car.

"Mom?" Tally called softly as she tapped on the door. A light shone behind the curtain. All the other rooms were dark and she assumed other people were asleep.

Nancy Holt answered the door and gathered her two children in her arms, hugging them so tightly they had trouble breathing. Inside the room, Tally and her mom sat on the bed and Cole took the chair.

"Mom, what happened?" Cole asked.

Tally had never seen her mother looked this ghastly. Even in the dim light from one table lamp, she looked old, wrinkled, and pale. She sat with her shoulders hunched and her head sagging down, like she didn't have the strength to hold it up.

Nancy slowly shook her head. "I don't know where to start."

"Mom, can I get you something?" Cole asked. "Something to eat or drink?"

She sighed, as if this was the hardest decision she'd ever made. Tally could tell her mother was beyond weary.

"A Coke would be good," she finally said.

Nancy downed part of it from the can after Cole came back from the vending machine, then started to tell them what had happened.

"You need to know this and I need to tell someone. It's going to be hard, though." She took a breath. "Okay, I'll start.

"I got up to get some more pain pills. I think it was about two or two-thirty, something like that. When I couldn't locate them, I took your father's satchel into the bathroom and turned on the light. There was a piece of paper tucked in with everything and I pulled it out."

Tally sucked her breath in, knowing what was coming. She glanced at Cole and his eyes were riveted on their mom, waiting for her next words.

When she didn't continue, Tally couldn't contain herself. "What was it, Mom? Tell us what it was."

Nancy raised her head and looked from Tally to Cole. "It was awful. I knew whose writing it was."

"Whose?" Cole leaned forward.

"That awful man. Wendell Samson."

"Who?" Cole asked.

"Is he the one Dad showed me a picture of?" Tally asked.

"Who is he? What picture?" Cole added.

"To answer that, I have to go back, way back, and tell you some things I had hoped you would never find out."

Chapter 12

Nancy Holt paused before she continued. "Cole, could you get me another soda?"

Tally knew that talking must have made her thirsty. She had finished the whole can Cole had brought to her.

"I'll get it," Tally said.

She went outside and drew in a deep breath of the night air, taking a moment to pause on the balcony. A slight breeze stirred the palm tree fronds so that they chattered below her and the clean, strong chlorine smell of the pool wafted up. After a moment, she went to the vending machine and a Coke clanged down the chute. She hoped the people in the nearest room weren't awakened by the noise.

At the door, Tally had to hesitate. What was her mother about to tell her? Did she want to hear it?

After their mom had a sip, Cole spoke. "Mom, who is Wendell Samson?" he asked, his impatience barely contained.

"He worked for us in the hardware store."

"Hardware store?" Cole asked.

"Yes. This was a long time ago, when your dad and I were first married. I don't suppose we've ever told you about the store, have we? We pooled our resources with the Abrahams and bought a hardware store right after we got married. Fran and Lennie had been married for about a year. Bob and I both had insurance money from the deaths of our grandparents and the Abrahams had just sold their family ranch. The store had been a good business, making money and thriving, but the owner was getting older and didn't want to run it anymore. He had no children and his wife had passed away."

Her parents and the Abrahams in business together? Tally would never have imagined that in a million years. She listened, rapt, to this unknown history.

"It was going well from the beginning, we thought, though it was a struggle to get it off the ground. The owner before us had neglected the business for a few years. Another two or three years and we would have been making more than sufficient money. Wendell was one of our three employees. He stocked the shelves, unloaded the delivery trucks, and cleaned after hours.

"Lennie was the first to notice, since he was handling the finances."

"Notice what?" Cole was almost thrumming with impatience. Tally wanted her to get to the point, too.

"Merchandise was disappearing. Someone was stealing from us. Since at least one of the four of us was in the store at all times, we were fairly certain it wasn't customers. Wendell was the one who was there after hours more than anyone else. We employed two others to help with sales and stocking, a young man and a young woman, whose families we knew. They occasionally worked late, but Wendell did his janitor work after hours every day. Bob spent some of our meager earnings on a security camera and we found out it was Wendell. He was pilfering almost every night.

"So..." Nancy took a deep breath, then another swig of soda. "We fired him."

"But how does murder come into that?" Cole said, leaning closer and closer.

"Wendell was outraged. He cursed and screamed before he left, then, that night, he set fire to the store."

"Oh no!" Tally said. "Did it burn down?"

"Mostly," her mother went on. "No one noticed the flames until it was too late to save it. We got there much too late. It was an awful thing to see." She stared into the past, a haunted look in her eyes. "There were two horrible results. The young man, our employee, had been inside and got trapped by a falling piece of the ceiling and...died."

"So Wendell essentially murdered him," Cole said.

"Yes. And Wendell was caught on camera setting the fire. The camera was one of the few things not destroyed."

"You said there were two horrible results," Tally said. "What was the other one?"

"It was the fact that we were grossly underinsured," her mother said. "We couldn't afford to insure the place the way we should have. We would have been able to later, but couldn't right then. We lost everything. Wendell was convicted of manslaughter and sent to prison. Lennie rashly told his wife that *we* would provide for his family, but we couldn't. Wendell's wife had a stroke during the trial and ended up paralyzed on one side. His family was destitute. Lennie also told the family of the man who died that we would all take care of them. Lennie seemed to think we would have enough insurance to cover everything." Nancy fished a tissue out of her purse on the nightstand and wiped her tears and her nose.

"You were destitute, too, weren't you?" Tally asked.

"Yes, we all were. Lennie was a good carpenter and started working at that, doing odd jobs and building things for people. Bob and I started performing for money in Dallas, Austin, Houston, and other places, wherever we could. Then we had you, then you." She looked at Tally, then Cole. "Our tours were successful and we did well, eventually. So did Lennie and Fran. They bought the theater, built it up, then sold it."

"And now they both work there," Tally said. "What happened to the rest of the Samson family?"

"I sometimes feel guilty about that, but I guess they got by on welfare. Bob offered to send the widow of the man who died some money to help out, years later, when we had it to spare. Lennie did, too, but she turned all of us down. We never knew if that was from pride, or if she really didn't need help."

"So, the note in Dad's satchel?" Tally asked, remembering what started all of this.

Nancy gazed into space, a troubled expression on her face, lost in the awful past. "Wendell tried to blame the fire on Bob at the time. He sent a series of those blackmail attempts before he was arrested. He was trying to extort money from us. Money that we didn't have, that he thought we had. I have no idea why your father saved that one, carrying it around all these years.

"Anyway, when I found it a few hours ago, I blew my stack. I've been feeling so awful and that just hit me wrong. With this current murder and that awful note…I thought it was a stupid thing to have with him. What if the police searched us? I started screaming at him and he yelled back. We both have voices that carry and someone in another suite must have called the police. They came barreling through the door. We didn't hear them knocking—we were being so loud. Bob was holding the note. They saw it and jumped to the conclusion that it was about Fran's murder."

"Oh, Mom!" Tally hugged her mother. The loud altercation had brought about the very thing they all feared.

* * * *

Yolanda had worked hard all of Thursday morning on a trio of baskets for a fundraising auction at the local TV station. She deserved lunch out, so she flipped her door sign to *Closed*, delivered the baskets, and drove to an upscale local grill to indulge herself. She called Kevin to see if he could join her, but he was too busy to leave. It was not a bad thing that his business was busy, she thought, and wished hers would be just a little busier. But, for now, she deserved this break.

She took a seat on the patio and ordered a salad with bacon-wrapped shrimp. It was a favorite of hers on the rare occasions when she dined there.

The weather was hot. It was August, after all, but she loved the warmth. She munched her salad and sipped a glass of crisp white wine, almost feeling cool.

"Mind if I join you?"

Yolanda turned to see who was behind her. Shiny Peth. Looking around, she noticed that the patio was full. Shiny probably couldn't find another place to sit, Yolanda thought. It wasn't as if they were buddies.

"Go ahead. I'm almost finished, then y'all can have this spot to yourself."

Shiny took the other chair at the round tabletop and a server appeared almost immediately.

When her own glass of white wine came, she raised it to clink with Yolanda. "To Fran Abraham," she said.

"To Fran?" Yolanda was puzzled. "What do you mean?"

"May she rest in peace," she rasped. "Or, maybe I should say, I'm so glad you're gone, Frannie."

Yolanda realized that this wasn't Shiny's first drink of the day. "May she rest in peace," Yolanda added. She hadn't liked the woman, but couldn't be glad that she—or anyone else—was dead.

"It couldn't have happened to a better person." Shiny took a sip, then raised her glass high, sloshing wine over the side to drip onto the white tablecloth.

Yolanda had no reply to that. She started shoveling her salad into her mouth so she could leave as soon as possible. With dismay, she noted that half her salad remained. Maybe if she picked out the bacon-wrapped shrimp and left the rest she could finish sooner.

"That looks good," Shiny said, eyeing Yolanda's salad. "I would never eat shrimp, though. You wanna know why?"

Yolanda raised her eyebrows instead of answering, not wanting to encourage further drunken ravings. Besides, her mouth was full.

"Because *she* liked shrimp. Our precious Frances Abraham, knower of all, boss of the world, thorn in the side of everyone in our theater. That's who. *She* liked shrimp." Shiny leaned over the table, waving her wobbling glass perilously close to Yolanda's lap. "Aren't you glad she's dead? Isn't everyone?"

Shiny threw herself back in her seat, spilling the wine onto herself.

"Shiny, can I order y'all a cup of coffee?" Yolanda asked, not knowing what else to say.

"I'm celebrating. Can't you see that? The woman told me not to come back. She threw me out of the community theater. And why? Because I caught her husband's eye. I'm not the first one to do that. He said I was pretty and I went with it. What's wrong with that? She didn't want him. At least not for the things that a husband does." A sly look came over Shiny's slack face.

Yolanda shoved the last shrimp into her mouth and rose. She would pay inside. She had to leave this lunatic.

"Leaving already? Mind if I finish your salad?"

"No, go ahead." It was mostly lettuce. Could that sober a person up? She wondered.

After she was well away from Shiny Peth, she began to wonder if the woman had murdered Fran. Was a guilty conscience the reason she was so drunk at a few minutes past noon?

Chapter 13

When there was a lull in the early afternoon, Lily approached Tally.

"Can I show you something?" Lily said, her face full of expectation and energy.

"Sure," Tally said. If it was something good, she wanted to know about it.

"In your office?"

Puzzled, Tally led the way.

"I need you to log your computer on. To the internet," Lily said with a smile.

Tally did so with Lily hovering over her shoulder.

"Go to oldetymesweets.com, all one word." Lily almost vibrated with excitement.

"Okay." Tally was smiling, too. She couldn't help it. When she opened the page, she was met with enticing pictures of her shop, the address and phone number displayed, with a map to click on for directions. She read the text: *Come in for a sweet surprise. Leave with your taste buds happy.* At the bottom, Tally Holt was listed as the owner.

"This is wonderful, Lily." Tally jumped up and clasped her. She had done this so quickly. What a treasure Lily was!

* * * *

It was midafternoon when Tally looked out the front window to see a couple across the street having difficulty making headway. It looked like the man was supporting a stumbling woman. Tally couldn't tell if they were both drunk, or if maybe the woman was the only one inebriated and the man was helping her walk. A potential customer who apparently couldn't read the ingredients printed on the box of Clark Bars waved it in front of her, so she turned her attention to selling her products. Tally patiently read the ingredients, then the woman huffed out of the store because the candy contained sugar. Tally was glad she hadn't had to read the ingredients of all the packages to her. They all contained sugar. They were candy, after all.

She had to shake her head that the woman expected vintage candies to be sugar-free.

For some reason, Allen popped into her head. She hadn't called him back the night before. She couldn't have—she'd been dealing with all the trouble going on with her parents. It had been such a long, exhausting day. But he hadn't called her, either. She checked her phone. No, he hadn't called. Well, they were both busy. And she was preoccupied.

The next time she looked out the front window, no more than a minute later, the couple was on her side of the street, walking past the shop. She was surprised to see that the woman was Shiny Peth. She didn't recognize the man and she barely recognized Shiny, for that matter. Shiny usually had the posture of a model, holding her head high and walking confidently. This Shiny was staggering, her head lolling forward with each awkward, labored step.

Tally's cell pinged with a text from Yolanda.

Did you just see Shiny? She was drunk at noon and it looks like she's in worse shape now

Shiny must have passed Yolanda's place just before she reached Tally's shop. She texted back: *Who is the guy?*

No idea

What was going on? How did Yolanda know for sure Shiny was drunk an hour ago? Tally had to talk to Yolanda.

"Lily, can you take over for a couple of minutes? I'll be right back." Without waiting for an answer, Tally zipped out the front door. She stopped and watched the couple stumble and trudge up the street and around the corner. Then she hurried to Yolanda's place and barged in.

Bella's Baskets held a record number of patrons. Tally was glad to see that for Yolanda's sake, but how could she collect gossip with all those people there? She pulled Yolanda to the back of the one-room shop, leaving Raul to handle the business for a few minutes.

"What do you mean, Shiny was drunk at noon? Where? How do you know?"

Yolanda told her about her interrupted lunch and about Shiny sitting with her, complaining about Fran, even celebrating her death.

"You know, I saw her around the theater soon after Fran died," Yolanda said. "And the way she acted at the reception, hanging on Lennie all night…I think she's having an affair with him."

"I'm pretty sure she was. That would be a good reason for Fran to ban her from the theater. I couldn't even blame Fran for that. But what's with this sudden drinking problem? Have you seen her do this before?"

"No, never. Do you think she has a guilty conscience?"

"You mean, because she…killed Fran?"

They looked at each other in silence. Tally didn't want Shiny to have killed Fran, but the fact was that someone had. She would rather it were Shiny than her father. "Who was the guy holding her up just now?"

"I don't know." Yolanda frowned. "I think I've seen him somewhere, but can't remember where."

Tally walked back to her shop deep in thought, jostling the crowds on the sidewalk, and not paying much attention to what she was doing. Shiny and the guy were nowhere to be seen now. What if Shiny had killed Fran? From what Yolanda said, Shiny despised Fran and had for quite a while. Lily had said that, too. But Fran had been killed from poison in the Whoopie Pies. How could Shiny have done that?

When Tally got back to her shop, she methodically—and casually, she hoped—took each employee aside and asked what she thought of Shiny Peth.

Molly Kelly thought she was beautiful and wanted to look like her.

"I even told my boyfriend that," she said. "I told him I wanted to look just like Shiny Peth. She's like…together, you know?"

"She is, I agree." Except for right now. Molly hadn't, apparently, seen her stagger past the shop.

"My boyfriend is great, though. He says he likes me just the way I am."

That was the first Tally had heard of a boyfriend. "Who are you seeing?"

"Howie. He's the owner of Howie's Garage." Pride shone in her bright blue eyes as she said it.

"He sounds like a catch. I'd hang onto him." Tally remembered Howie helping Allen Wendt out once when he needed a mechanic. Howie had come to his rescue quickly and efficiently.

"How did Shiny get along with Fran Abraham, do you know?"

"I don't hang around those people much. I just know her from seeing her around town. But nobody much liked Fran, did they?"

"I guess not."

A little later Tally was able to corner Lily Vale. Lily had danced for Fran, so she should know the theater people. "Do you know Shiny Peth very well?" she asked.

"Not really. I mean, I know her to talk to, but we're not buds or anything. I know she's talented. I've seen her perform. Why?"

"I just wondered."

"Why?"

Darn, Lily was too perceptive. Tally remembered Lily talking about her earlier. "You said Fran blackballed her from the theater, right?"

"She sure did."

"Was Shiny upset about that?"

"Maybe. I think Fran was more upset with Shiny, though. Shiny was making a play for Fran's husband, Len, is what I heard. Well, I saw it, too. It was obvious. Then, at your party, she was all over him. She came in with him, practically, and hung on him all night."

Tally thought that gave Fran more motive to murder Shiny than it gave Shiny motive to murder Fran. If Shiny was focused on Len, how was she able to sneak poison into the confections?

Tally would keep Shiny on her mental suspect list, but not at the top, for sure.

A couple of things continued to bother Tally about the poisoning. One was the fact that her father's fingerprints were on the serving platter. Her helpers' prints were also on it, but that was to be expected. If someone else were the poisoner, more fingerprints should be there.

Another question bugged her. Did the poisoner have an intended victim? If so, how was that supposed to be accomplished? The treats were being served by multiple people to everyone there. If a random poisoner were at work, would that make any sense? Tally shuddered at the thought that maybe more people could have died that night.

Chapter 14

Tally sped home after work to feed Nigel. She was on foot, since she had walked to work that morning instead of driving. The day was still lovely, but she didn't stop to appreciate it.

"Why am I so excited?" she asked the husky cat as he, ignoring her, chowed down on his kibble. "He's probably going to say he's moving out of town. He keeps threatening."

Nigel glanced up at her and blinked.

"Oh, you're right. Allen has never met you. He called this afternoon and said he wanted to see me tonight. It seems out of the blue. I didn't know he was in town. I don't know why I'm nervous. No, not nervous. Excited. Okay, maybe a little nervous."

She quit babbling and left Nigel, busy at his din-din bowl, and went to her closet to go through her clothing. It was, of course, hot out. August in Texas was always hot out. Would he want to eat outside? The Eatery Island had a nice patio, but she would rather not sweat onto her dinner. She would try to get him to eat inside—if there was room. Just to be safe, she chose a sundress with a matching short jacket. Outside would be sweltering hot, but inside, in true Texas tradition, would be icicle cold.

When they got to the Eatery, sure enough, first available would be the patio dining area or terrace. It was available after only half a drink from the bar, which was nice. They had tried making small talk at the crowded bar, but it was too noisy to hear anything below shouting volume.

After being seated at the edge of the area, near the short wrought iron railing, she shed the jacket. Glad that she'd stuck a new packet of tissues in her purse, she discreetly mopped her forehead and the back of her neck, then studied the menu.

"What are you having?" she asked Allen, not wanting to outspend him. She wasn't sure if this was Dutch treat or not. She wished she knew if they had a relationship or not.

"I always have the same thing," he said. "Steak and a Caesar."

A soft breeze stirred the warm air and made the patio almost pleasant. Tally was grateful that the piped-in music was low and unobtrusive. That made it easy to talk and to hear each other. And everyone else, it turned out.

The server who had seated them came up behind Allen. "Is this table acceptable?" he asked...Ionia Goldenberger, of all people. She was with her husband. Tally hadn't met him, but had seen him around town and knew who he was. He was a CPA for a firm in Fredericksburg, a distinguished-looking gray-haired man in slacks and a white shirt tonight. She had only seen him in suits before this. Ionia wore a swishy long-ish dress of dark blues and blacks.

Ionia was the one who, Tally knew, had been spreading rumors about Fran and trying to get her fired. Tally agreed with Ionia that she would have made a better theater director than Fran, but the organization was run by a board. It had been, ever since the Abrahams sold it to an out-of-towner who owned several small theaters around Texas.

Now, with Fran dead, would they give Ionia the job she had wanted for so long?

Their server came to take their order. Allen ordered a rather nice bottle of red wine and they both asked for steaks, splitting the large Caesar salad the place was famous for. It was shaping up to be a lovely, relaxing evening.

She heard Ionia and her husband discussing what to order. Ionia's voice drifted over to them. "Don't be silly. You know I never touch sugar or white flour."

"Are you doing okay with—" Allen started to ask her.

She shushed him and whispered, "Wait a sec. I have to hear this." She concentrated on what Ionia was saying to her husband.

"That's not true. It's not never," he said.

"Hardly ever," she answered. "When is the last time you saw me eat sugar? Or white flour?"

"Valentine's Day?"

Ionia giggled and gave him a coquettish look, Tally deduced from the back of her head as she ducked her chin. "You got me. I did eat that candy. But not since then."

Allen was looking at her sideways with the beginnings of an annoyed frown.

"Sorry," Tally said. "I wanted to hear something. What were you saying?"

"Nothing important, apparently."

Was Allen pouting? Good grief. "No, I want to know what you want to tell me."

"But you only want to know after you've finished eavesdropping on strangers in the restaurant."

Tally kept her voice as low as she could, since the Goldenbergers were right there, at the next table. There was a generous amount of room between the tables, but, after all, she could easily overhear them. "They're not strangers. The woman knew Fran, who died in my shop, and I wanted to see if maybe—"

"Maybe? Maybe what?"

Now she lowered her voice even more. "If maybe she could be the one who killed her."

"Oh, for…" He didn't seem to think much of her sleuthing method.

"Allen, the police think my *father* did it. I'm getting desperate."

"It's not attractive, Tally."

"Attractive?"

"Spying on other people. It isn't right."

It was Tally's turn to pout. She wasn't spying—she was eavesdropping. Ionia was having a public conversation. It wasn't like Tally was tapping her phone.

"Well, anyway," he said, "I'm leaving again tomorrow. I have a long haul to the coast."

Was that what he'd wanted to tell her? She didn't think so. "How long will you be gone?"

"I don't know. A while."

The rest of the meal was not pleasant. They were both sullen and short with each other and Tally was relieved when she got back through her front door and was alone with Nigel. She sat on the couch and curled up with the purring, nonjudgmental fur ball. And cried. Maybe she *was* starting to care for Allen. Otherwise, why was she so upset they were on the outs?

When she calmed down and wiped her last sniffle, she turned her attention to what Ionia had been saying. If what she said was true, or mostly true—except for Valentine's Day—she would not have eaten any of Tally's wares at the reception. So it wouldn't be suspicious if she passed them up. Did she make sure that Fran got some?

Tally shook her head at her own thought. Nobody had had to force Fran to eat the Whoopie Pies. Her servers had told her that Fran gobbled them down whenever they were offered to her. Two or three times, Tally gathered. Did everyone know what an intense sweet tooth she had? That she was such a glutton for sweets? Probably. That would make her easy to poison. Maybe it was just luck that no one else was poisoned. She was getting nowhere thinking about Ionia and the murder. She turned her thoughts to wondering how her mother was doing.

It wasn't that late, not yet 9:30. She called her parents to see if she could drop by to see them.

Her father answered the phone. "I think you should come over. Your mother's in a state."

Now what?

"Dad, you're there! Not in jail."

"No, they questioned me and let me go. I don't think they have enough evidence."

Tally didn't like the sound of that. She would rather they didn't have *any* evidence. She dropped some cool, soothing artificial tears into her eyes to mask the fact that she'd been crying, and drove to the hotel.

After she rapped on the door and her father let her in, she was alarmed at her mother's appearance. Had she relapsed? She looked even worse than the last time Tally saw her. She gave her dad a long hug first, then turned to her mother.

"What's the matter, Mom?"

Cole was there, too, without Dorella. "She's gotten some bad news."

Tally waited for someone to tell her what was going on.

"He's out," her mother whispered. She looked like that was a tragic thing, whatever she meant.

"Out?" Tally echoed. "He?"

"That man," Cole said. "The one who burned down their store all those years ago."

"He escaped from prison?" Tally was alarmed. That man had no love for her parents. "Are they searching for him?"

"Yes, they called us to tell us he escaped." Her father's voice sounded reasonable and calm. "He managed to overpower a guard when the electricity went out during a recent storm. The sheriff called about a half an hour ago to tell us, since we're on the notification list."

"He didn't call right away?" Tally asked.

"He apologized," her father said. "He said he had a busy day with an interstate pileup and worked late tonight. I'm glad he called tonight and not tomorrow. The sooner we know, the better. But, he didn't call very soon."

"That man has it in for you, doesn't he? The one who escaped, not the sheriff," Tally asked, remembering the hostile note she'd found. The note that had caused so much trouble for her poor dad.

"Is he in the area?" Cole asked. "The prison isn't that far away, is it?"

"It's up at Abilene, about three hours away," Bob said. "The thing is, the sheriff admitted he got out last week. He should have called then."

"Last week!" Tally cried. "He could be here now. He could have killed Fran."

"That's exactly what I was thinking," her dad said.

Tally studied her mother. She was so thin, her collarbones were clearly visible. Was that new? "Mom, are you eating enough?"

"Tally," her dad said. "She doesn't feel well enough yet. She's doing the best she can be doing. She's just recently quit throwing up."

"I'm feeling much better, dear," Nancy said to her daughter. "I ate a sandwich tonight, both halves. That's the most solid food I've kept down since I got sick. I've been taking teensy bites of everything, but I ate the whole sandwich all at once. I think I'll start feeling much better now. I'm actually hungry today."

Tally tried to decide if her mother really looked better, or if she was just seeing her more critically tonight. It was late. They were probably all tired. And they were all worried about that man Wendell being on the loose.

Chapter 15

Tally slept poorly that night. A brief, violent thunderstorm interrupted the slumbering peace of Fredericksburg in the wee hours of the morning. She'd been fitfully dozing until then, but after the furor of the storm, she lay awake, stewing about the danger her parents were in and worrying about how to find the real killer.

When it was time to go to work she decided to walk to work off some of her nervous energy and worry. The storm had strewn the sidewalks with crepe myrtle petals. A vision of her as a bride, walking through rose petals to an altar, sprang—unwanted—into her mind.

Ha, she told herself. As if that would ever happen. She might dress up as a bride, but who would be waiting at the front of the church for her? Who would be her other half, the way her father was for her mother? They loved each other so much, worried about each other, took care of each other. On occasion they could finish each other's sentences. Tally couldn't imagine that ever happening between her and anyone she had ever known.

She'd seen Detective Jackson Rogers casually a few times, but how could she ever get close to someone who would suspect her father of murder? Last night she'd thought of Allen as a romantic partner, but was he? They had nothing in common and she wasn't sure he would still be in town from one week to the next. There was no one.

As she turned the corner to approach Tally's Olde Tyme Sweets from the front, she looked up. She was surprised to see Mrs. Gerg standing there.

"Yoo-hoo!" the older woman called when Tally was still half a block away. "I'm over here."

Tally wondered why she hadn't come to her house, as usual, but Mrs. Gerg soon explained.

"This gigantic neighborhood sale started early this morning and I got there as soon as it was opening, lucky me. I wanted to get this to you right away." She held a small, oblong box out to Tally.

She knew what it was, of course. Another cheap necklace. Tally said thank you and took the box. When she opened it and saw the contents, she was glad she had already thanked Mrs. Gerg. She was speechless. The necklace was made of such cheap metal it appeared plastic. A large, openwork heart dangled on a dull silver chain. The word *MOM* was spelled across it in fake blue diamonds. Mom? She couldn't help but give Mrs. Gerg a puzzled look.

The woman beamed. "It's for you! You're a mom now."

"I am?" she croaked. For a moment, she thought she had lost track of reality. Maybe she had had a baby and Mrs. Gerg knew about it and she was suffering from amnesia.

"You are. You have a little fur baby. Well, a big fur baby."

Tally nodded, still mostly speechless. It was a relief to find out what in the heck the woman was talking about. "I am, you're right. Nigel is my new baby. Thanks so much."

"I knew you'd love it!" Mrs. Gerg trundled away, smiling broadly.

At least the necklaces didn't take up much room in her dresser drawer. The collectible, ornamental boxes Mrs. Gerg used to give her had taken up a lot of space.

Shiny Peth came into the shop soon after Tally unlocked the front door to the public. She was seeing entirely too much of this woman lately. Tally happened to be the only one in the room. The others, Lily and Molly, were fetching merchandise from the refrigerator and the pantry to fill the display cases.

"Are you open?" Shiny asked.

"Yes, the sweets will be out in a moment," Tally said. "Is there something special you want?" She stood behind the empty glass cases, ready to help arrange the goodies in them.

"Yes, there is. I'll need something marvelous for tonight. Lennie and I are celebrating."

"That's nice," Tally said, hearing how lame her words were as soon as they left her mouth. "I mean, congratulations. What are you celebrating?"

Shiny dangled her left hand in front of Tally by way of answering. Tally couldn't miss the gigantic diamond ring. It caught a ray of sunshine from the front window and flung it in glittering shards across the walls and ceiling of the shop.

"Wow." Tally was stunned.

Molly and Lily entered the room and echoed, even more emphatically, "Wow!" Molly stopped in mid-stride and stared. Lily kept going toward the display case with her tray, but her head swiveled all the way there, sneaking one look after another at the huge rock.

"You're engaged?" Tally said. Since Lennie's wife was dead, that had to be legal. But she hadn't been dead very long. "Just now?"

Shiny leaned close to Tally. "Actually, he gave me the ring weeks ago. I was going to start wearing it as soon as the divorce came through."

"He was getting a divorce?"

Shiny shrugged. "No reason not to. He said he couldn't stand her another minute."

A divorce, Tally thought, would cost a lot more than a burial service. She vowed to make sure Detective Rogers knew about this liaison, and about how long it had been going on. Definitely before Fran died. How she wished she could remember every detail from that night! She wished she knew where each person was moment by moment, but she'd been so busy running the gathering that she hadn't kept track of every individual. She'd been trying to get through the evening, keeping track of Molly and Lily and Greer—when she could—hoping she wouldn't run out of things for people to eat, and worrying about Yolanda's family. Tally drummed her fingers on top of the glass case, then stopped, aware of the hollow noise she was making.

Molly finally unfroze and handed her tray of Mary Janes to Tally, still unable to take her eyes off Shiny's ring.

Lily, having stocked a shelf and gone back for more merchandise, came through the kitchen door with another pile of boxed goods to arrange. Shiny had stopped sticking her left arm out, but was holding her hand up, ostentatiously displaying the ring to herself.

Molly nudged Lily and whispered, "Get a load of that."

Lily didn't say anything and she continued her task, but wore an expression of disbelief.

Tally wondered if either of them had ever seen a diamond that large. She certainly hadn't. It looked to be at least ten carats. If it was real, Tally wondered how much it had cost Lennie. Had he gotten insurance money from Fran's death already? No, he surely couldn't have. Could he? Maybe someone gave him credit on the hope he would get it. At any rate, would buying her this ring and thereby cementing the relationship, presumably, be a good motive to murder his wife? Maybe there was enough motive without the ring. Shiny was an attractive woman, a real catch. Tally wasn't sure what Shiny saw in Lennie. He was not only older, but rough around the edges compared to her.

Tally drummed her fingers in thought, again stopping when her nails clicked on the glass display case. Lennie wasn't that bad-looking for his age, she had to admit. She probably thought of him negatively because she closely associated him with Fran—two old, wrinkled people. Lennie still had a lot of hair on his head, if one liked that. He was also robust and strong and didn't have too much of a potbelly. He was older than Shiny by thirty, maybe forty years. That was a lot, but it happened all the time. If she were thinking cynically, she knew some women liked to snare older men because they wouldn't last that long.

"Did Randy give that to you?" Lily asked.

Tally whirled to stare at Lily. Who was Randy?

Shiny took a step back and her expression soured. "No. This is from Lennie."

"What about Randy?" Lily persisted.

Tally realized Lily had been out of the room when Shiny said she was engaged to Len.

"Nothing about Randy," Shiny snapped. "He doesn't know about this yet. You'd better not tell him, either. Tally, I think I'd like to have two-dozen chocolate-covered caramels, a dozen Mary Janes, and a pound of mint fudge." She pointedly turned her back to Lily and waited while Tally wrapped her purchases.

After Shiny paid and stalked out, Tally had to ask. "Who's Randy?" she said to Lily.

"That's her boyfriend. They've been seeing each other for at least a year."

Interesting. She wondered if Randy was the man who had been helping her walk along the sidewalk yesterday, propping her up, when Shiny was so drunk. Yolanda hadn't mentioned that a man had been with her at lunch, but he was soon after that.

Chapter 16

During a midmorning lull, Tally remembered her mother telling her about the family of the man who died in the fire Wendell set in the hardware store, about how Lennie promised them he would take care of them as well as the Samson family, but couldn't provide for any of them because they didn't have insurance. It was a long time ago, but she wondered what had happened to the family of the man who perished. Wouldn't they have a great deal of animosity against Lennie, and probably Fran and her parents, too? She wanted to find out more about the backgrounds of her employees. Did it make sense that one of them would seek employment with her in order to get at her parents? Maybe it did. They were all initially hired to help at the reception, which she had told them was for her parents. Would they know that Fran and Lennie would be there, too? Probably not, since even she hadn't known they would be coming.

Unless…one of her employees was the daughter of that poor family and decided to make sure the Abrahams would be there. That wouldn't be hard to do. Lily knew them from dancing at the theater. Greer or Molly could have made sure to get the word to them…somehow.

"What's that noise?" a customer asked, looking around in Tally's direction.

Darn, she was drumming her nails again. She plunged her hands into her smock pockets.

She took a break midafternoon and went to her office to search online for news of the old fire. The local paper had archived editions, but the organization wasn't ideal. She knew the approximate year and was able to give some date parameters in searching the files. Eventually, she found the initial story with a picture of the burned structure. It was almost leveled.

One brick wall stood—the rest of the place had collapsed. She shuddered to think that a person had lost his life there.

The accounts didn't release the name of the deceased until several days later: Owen Herd. It didn't list any relatives. So she started searching the obituaries to see who the surviving family members were.

"Ms. Holt," called Lily, rapping on her closed office door. "Can you help out?"

Tally closed down her computer and rushed to the front to help cut through the chaos of a suddenly extremely crowded store. A glance through the window explained the rush. A tour bus was parked directly in front, idling at the curb, and the bus tourists were hurrying to make purchases and get on their way.

It gave Tally a lift to realize that her shop was on a tour! She made a mental note of the company, Texas Treasure Tours, so she could contact them to ask if this would be a regular thing and, if it would, maybe they could give her a schedule. For the time being, she was afraid her place would sell out before everyone was satisfied.

After the crowd climbed back into the bus and it puffed away, the display cases were decimated. The refrigerator was, too.

"I'll run back and start making more...what should I make first?" Lily asked.

Tally surveyed the shelves and decided that she should concentrate on Mallomars, Twinkies, and Clark Bars. All the Mallomars were gone and there were less than a half dozen of the other two.

Tally didn't get back to her online research until the shop closed at seven. No sooner did she open her computer than her cell phone rang.

"Tally?" Yolanda sounded stressed. "I need to talk. Are y'all still at work?"

Yolanda was in her own shop, so Tally closed hers up and walked over to Bella's Baskets.

She found Yolanda on the verge of tears, twisting one of her dark brown curls tightly, over and over until Tally was afraid she would yank it out.

* * * *

Yolanda was happy to see her best friend. She'd had such a horrid day. Tally held out her arms and the two women hugged for a long time.

"It's your parents again, I assume?" Tally said.

Yolanda nodded, sure she would burst into sobs if she tried to speak. She pointed to her flower cooler, where they both knew there was always a bottle of white wine chilling. Tally fetched the wine and two stemmed glasses from one of her supply cupboards.

By the time Tally had poured the wine and Yolanda had had a sip, she was able to talk. "Vi and Eden want to come up tomorrow and my parents don't even want them to stay at the house."

Tomorrow would be Saturday, not a day off for Yolanda or for Tally, but her parents would be relaxing at home, probably swimming and having their usual cookout. A perfect setup for hosting friends of their daughter. Unless Yolanda was terribly busy and had a good excuse, she was always expected for dinner on Saturday night. Whenever Violetta was in town, she was expected also.

"Vi has never stayed anywhere but at our house when she visits. That's just mean to exclude Eden."

"What did they say, exactly? That Vi can stay there, but Eden can't?"

"No," wailed Yolanda. "They don't want either one of them at the house. Not even for dinner. Papa said they could come for either cocktails or dessert."

"What? That's crazy."

"It's mean. It's cruel. It's like they're disowning their daughter." Yolanda, in her mind was going to say "their favorite daughter," but didn't want to bring that up just now.

Over the last few days, since Vi had had her coming out, Yolanda felt the fierce sibling rivalry she had always held onto toward her sister becoming less and less important, fading to the background of the more dramatic, current events in Vi's life.

"Is your sister still going to come to Fredericksburg?" Tally asked. "I don't think I would."

"Vi asked me what to do. I'll tell her that. To not come. They'll eventually have to accept that she's gay. Won't they?"

"I hope so."

"I mean, they know she's gay. They'll have to accept her as she is."

"I'm so sorry about all this," Tally said and they hugged some more.

After Tally left, Yolanda sat, immobile, for ten minutes. Then she decided. She wasn't going to show up, either. She would eat at her own home. Or go out. If her place were bigger, she would tell Vi to bring Eden and stay with her, but it would be too crowded. Now, should she tell her parents she wouldn't be there? Or just let them find out when she didn't show up?

Chapter 17

It wasn't yet eight o'clock and the library would be open another hour, on summer hours, so Tally headed there from Yolanda's. Singing tree frogs and chattering cicadas accompanied her on the three-block walk through the dense, warm air. The sun was setting, turning the fronts of the quaint buildings a brilliant pinking orange. Could there be a more beautiful place to live? she wondered, slowing to enjoy her short walk.

She ambled up the long sidewalk to the ancient brick building that always reminded her, a bit, of the Alamo in San Antonio. They both had the same pale, tan stone walls and similar rooflines with peaks and an elevated round center hump in the middle of the front.

When she got inside the library, she filled out a form for the friendly, smiling librarian and waited to receive permission to search the old newspaper articles. Now that she knew what she was looking for, and the dates, it should be fairly easy to find the obituary and, she hoped, some family members' names. And much easier in the library archives than online, she hoped.

She sat and scoured the pages, at last finding a short death notice on Owen Herd. He was survived by his parents—that was sad—and his wife and four children. That was even sadder. They were all named Herd, of course. His wife was Nancy, the same as Tally's mother. The four children all had G names: Grace, George, Gina, and Geoff.

What would she find out if she kept searching? Would there be articles about them? She covered a month's worth of issues before the library began to close up, without finding an article about any of the rest of the Herd family. After a slow walk home through the darkening streets, she continued her quest on her home computer. When she came up empty, she started looking for information about the arsonist, Wendell Samson. She found his trial was covered extensively. One mention was made of the Herd family, and that was that they had moved out of town. There was no mention of where they had moved to. She had hit a dead end on the Herds.

It was late. Nigel had dozed off after trying to disturb Tally's searching as hard as he could. After he'd been fed, he brought a stuffed mouse toy to Tally, wanting her to play. He even leaped onto her keyboard with it in his mouth at one point. She was concentrating so hard that she didn't even realize he'd given up, but he was snoozing on the couch now.

Tally realized she was ravenous. She slapped together a sandwich, sank onto the couch next to Nigel, and flicked on the TV, to munch and watch something mindless.

Her brain strayed from the inane comedy, though. She couldn't help but want to keep trying to explore the trail. It was true, she had hit a dead end, but the family was somewhere. They couldn't have vanished. What if they had moved away, then moved back? What if they had changed their names? Or what if one of them had changed her name? Maybe from Grace to…Greer? That driver's license had to be altered.

Maybe her parents knew what had happened to them. Why hadn't she thought of asking them before she spent all that time on useless research? It was late now. She would talk to them tomorrow.

In the morning, Tally called her mother before she set out for the shop. Nancy Holt had known their names all along.

"We contacted them a couple of times right after the fire," Nancy said. "Bob and Len both tried to offer them some financial assistance, but Mrs. Herd turned it down. I thought, myself, that our offers weren't nearly enough money to make any difference to them. I don't think I would have taken it, either."

"When did they move? Do you know where they went?"

"One day they were just gone, Mrs. Herd and all the children. A few years later, when Bob and I started making money on our tours, your dad hired a private detective to try to find them, but there was no trace. We wanted to finally make things right for them. We never could. That has bothered me for years."

"Thanks, Mom."

"Why do you want to know all this? What are you thinking?"

Tally heard her dad's voice in the background and a door closing.

"Just set it there, Bob," her mother said. "We can eat in a minute. I'm talking to Tally."

He had probably gone out and gotten them breakfast, Tally thought.

"Mom, I just thought—maybe, well, is it possible that Mrs. Herd or, more likely, one of the children, decided to even the score finally?"

"You mean… You mean you think one of them killed Fran?"

"And tried to kill the rest of you."

"How could that be? Wouldn't we know they were back? Wouldn't Len and Fran know?"

"Do you think you would recognize any of the children, grown up?"

"I know all their names."

"Names can be changed."

"So they can," her mother agreed.

Her mother admitted, before Tally ended the call, that she probably wouldn't know any of the Herd children on sight. She might not even recognize Mrs. Herd now.

Around midmorning, Lily begged Tally to call Greer. "We really need her, Ms. Holt. I've seen two customers get impatient and leave because I was too busy to wait on them."

Greer was supposed to work Saturdays, the way Tally had set things up originally, when Molly and Greer were sharing the part-time responsibilities. Tally hadn't rescheduled Molly for additional time when she fired Greer. One Lily equaled one Molly, plus one Greer, Tally knew, but those were who she had to work with, unless she hired more help. She gave in and called Greer. To her surprise, she reached her right away. Greer sounded delighted to be coming back to work. To Tally's amazement, she was at the shop within half an hour.

Greer worked hard and she and Lily made an efficient team, for once. Maybe that was what Greer had needed, the scare of losing her job. Tally wouldn't count on her being on time every day, but she admitted it might start happening.

All through that day at work, Tally tried not to look at her employees suspiciously, but it was hard. She *was* suspicious. By the end of the day, she had decided she would have to be methodical. She would have to delve deeply into the lives of each young woman, one at a time. Lily would be first.

Tally didn't want to stay in her office late again, so she stuck all the employee application paperwork into a grocery bag that sugar and flour had been delivered in and took them home.

Nigel was thrilled to see her. He ran to greet his mistress almost like a puppy dog.

"You're a fun little guy, you know that?" She leaned down and rubbed between his soft ears, setting off a roaring purr. "Do you love me or do you just want food? I'll probably never know."

She fed the cat, made herself a salad, and dumped the applications onto her kitchen table. She had decided to start with Lily Vale, so she looked at hers first. Lily was fresh out of high school, but had an employment history, nevertheless. She'd worked summers since she was sixteen, two waitress jobs and a clerk in a fast-food store. There was nothing about her dancing in her résumé, but she had said she danced at the theater for musicals that Fran had put on and seemed to know quite a bit about Fran and Lennie. They would have been together for weeks of rehearsals.

Lily was local, having lived in Fredericksburg and gone to school in town her whole short life. Only two addresses were listed. The first was, presumably, her parents' house. Tally looked up the second. It was an apartment, she was surprised to see. Tally would have expected her to still live with her parents. She was young to be living on her own. Maybe she had a roommate or something. There was no way of telling.

Tally pondered the rest of the scanty information she had on Lily. Nothing pointed to her being a Herd child, unless the first address was false. When she looked it up online, it was a pleasant three-bedroom house that hadn't changed hands, according to the real estate sites, in more than twenty years. How could she find out if the Vales lived there?

There was a knock on her door, as if in answer to her question. It turned out that it *was* the answer.

Mrs. Gerg stepped into Tally's living room as she handed over a small bag.

"This looks brand-new, doesn't it? Look, there's even a price tag."

Tally drew a double strand of pearls from the bag. Nothing she would ever wear, but they could have been valuable. The tag had the name of a national jewelry chain store and the amount of…$659. Tally stared at Mrs. Gerg after seeing the tag. She didn't want to accept such an expensive item from her.

"See? I got them for almost nothing. It's a divorce and she left him for another man." Mrs. Gerg leaned close and whispered, even though they were in Tally's living room with the front door closed to the street. "It's that trashy couple down the block and across the street from me. I never liked them. So now the man is selling everything that belongs to her."

Was that legal? Tally wondered. Or was it theft? She would hang onto these in case the police wanted them back some day. She realized that the address Lily had given Tally for her parents' house was across the street from Mrs. Gerg. It was worth a try.

"Do you know a couple named Vale in your neighborhood?"

"Oh yes, I do. Or I did. They moved away. They were very nice people."

Alarms went off for Tally. "When did they move?"

"Oh, let's see. It was a while ago. Maybe a year? Their daughter, Lily, moved into an apartment with her cousin Amy, the daughter of Mrs. Vale's brother. They're almost the same age. Amy's family lives on a ranch outside town."

Tally wanted to sit Mrs. Gerg down and quiz her about the other two women, but needed to do some homework on them first. She thanked Mrs. Gerg profusely for the necklace and for the information.

"Why do you want to know? Oh, I know. She's working for you, isn't she?"

"Yes. She's a good employee. I'm very happy with her."

"I should say so. She's an angel. Never been in trouble a minute in her life."

After Mrs. Gerg left, it occurred to Tally that she should, in the future, probably run all prospective employees past Mrs. Gerg before she hired them.

When Tally saw Allen's number pop up on her phone as she was bedding down, she considered not answering it. But that would be stupid. And juvenile.

He sounded perfectly relaxed. And friendly. "Hey, Tally. It's good to hear your voice. I feel like I'm so far away."

"You've only been gone two days, right? But, yeah, it's good to hear you, too."

"Look, I'm sorry our date didn't go well. I want to make it up to you next time I'm in town."

"I guess it was my fault, too. It's just that—"

"I know, you're so concerned about your parents and what happened to Fran."

Something occurred to Tally. "Did you know her? Do you know the Abrahams?"

"Sure, I did work for them when I was doing the contracting, the handyman stuff."

She should have thought of that before. "What did you think of them?"

"Well, I liked Len a lot. Fran, not so much. Okay, not at all. I'm not the only one. No one could stand her."

"I wonder what made her so mean. I don't think she used to be that way. They were both friends and even business associates with my parents a long time ago, before I was born."

"Really? One thing that probably hardened Fran was the way Len ran around."

"He does have a roving eye, I'm learning."

"Both eyes. Plus other body parts. I don't know why she stayed with him."

"Or why he stayed with her."

"Oh, I know that part."

Tally sat up in bed. "You do?"

"I heard him complain about it. He was practically shacked up with the latest starlet. She was on him to leave Fran, but he and Fran had a prenup. He told her he couldn't afford a divorce. Fran would get everything. Their house, bank account, all of it."

They talked a bit more and ended with tender good nights. Tally figured killing Fran had to be considerably cheaper than divorcing her.

Chapter 18

In the morning, Tally decided to concentrate her research on Greer Tomson next. She was almost positive Greer had given her an altered driver's license. What would be the best way to handle that? Direct confrontation? First, though, she would look up her address.

She closed her office door and sat at the desk. Greer had only filled in one address on the form. When Tally put it into her computer and looked at the street view of the shabby apartment building, she was appalled. In appeared that Greer lived in abject poverty. Tally wondered if her mother— the one who was either dead or alive, depending on which story Greer was telling at the time—lived there, too. She was glad she had given the poor girl her job back, even if she wasn't a very good worker. Greer had listed her mother as her only reference. How did she expect to get away with saying she was dead? Tally should have noticed that.

Her application answers were odd for another reason, though, now that she stopped to think about it. The woman had had lots of jobs, having dropped out of high school a few years ago and worked since then. But none of the jobs had lasted very long. Had she been fired from them? All of them? Maybe she needed to be shown how to behave properly in a work situation.

It was Sunday. Molly was working and Tally had given Greer the day off, back to the original schedule. Molly was in the kitchen whipping up batches of candies as Tally started on payroll, still in her office.

"I hate to bother you," Molly said, sticking her head in the doorway. The hubbub of the busy shop poured in through the opening, borne on the smell of a new batch of peanut clusters. "But we're running low on peanuts. I need some more if I'm going to finish the peanut clusters."

Tally saved and closed her files. "I'll run get some."

"It's Sunday, Ms. Holt. Where you going to get them?"

"I'll have to use the grocery store. How much do you need?"

The amount for one batch wouldn't be too bad. It wouldn't break her bank. They were getting a shipment on Monday. It wouldn't take long at all and she would swing by the place where Greer lived to try to see if she actually lived there. Why hadn't she checked these things out before she hired them? She had trusted what they put on paper without verifying anything. Greer should also have given her references from her previous jobs, at least one or two. Tally was learning how to run a business the hard way—by doing it wrong.

She'd had it easy in Austin with her bakery. Her employees had all been hardworking and trustworthy—never a moment's trouble. Oh well, now she knew better. She'd been lucky in Austin.

After picking up the peanuts, she swung her little blue Chevy Sonic down the street where Greer lived. At the last moment, she worried about what to do if Greer saw her checking up on the address. This wasn't a part of town she usually—or ever—went to. If she got spotted, she could stretch the truth a bit and say it was a shortcut back to the shop. If she didn't say where she was coming from.

Some older people and few teenagers were sitting outside the buildings on the front steps of the multifamily dwellings. Maybe they didn't have air conditioning, poor souls. She slowed when she approached the middle of the block and searched the house numbers. Not every building had one, but the number she sought was displayed in big enough numbers to spot easily.

An elderly-looking woman sat in a wheelchair on the stoop, right outside the door. A younger woman bent over the older one, facing away from Tally. Even from the back, Tally could tell that the younger woman was Greer. Tally didn't dare stop, or go more slowly, but she was able to observe that the woman in the wheelchair looked like a stroke victim. One side of her face drooped and her left arm, held against her thin chest, was rigid and shriveled.

Tally kept going, thankful that Greer didn't turn around.

Her heart went out to Greer, living in such an awful place and, it seemed, tending a disabled relative. However, she still needed to talk to her about the falsified license. This wasn't something she had foreseen ever having to do as a business owner.

Poor Greer, but poor Tally, too.

* * * *

On Monday, the shop was lively. More lively than Tally wanted it to be. As soon as she unlocked the front door at ten o'clock, customers crowded in. They had been waiting outside. That gave her a warm feeling. What didn't give her a warm feeling, however, was that Greer hadn't shown up for work yet. Lily, as usual, was in place bright and early. Tally could have been doing some baking in the back at the moment, but needed to help wait on people in Greer's absence.

Greer strolled through the front door fifteen minutes late. Half of the first influx had already bought goods and left, so Tally took a deep breath and asked Greer to see her in the office for a few minutes.

Greer followed her into the small space and sat as soon as she was in. Tally wondered if she was perpetually exhausted from taking care of the woman she assumed was her disabled mother. She couldn't let her pity get in the way of bringing up what was an illegal, deceptive act.

"Greer," Tally said, opening the file folder that was waiting on her desk, rustling through the paperwork, and picking up the photocopy of her driver's license, "can you explain this?"

She barely glanced at it. "It's my driver's license."

"Do you see anything wrong with it? Take a close look."

Leaning forward, her eyes wide, she took another glance. "Nope, that's it. It's mine."

Tally dropped the copy of the license onto the folder and sat back, looking Greer in the eyes. "It's fake."

"What?" Greer pasted surprise all over her face. "What do you mean? They sent me a fake license?" She looked down, avoiding Tally's eyes.

"No, Greer. You changed it. I want to know why."

Greer kept staring at her own lap. A frown line made a fleeting appearance above her nose. After a considerable silence, she looked up, her lips tight. "I'm not supposed to tell anyone."

"Okay. Not supposed to tell anyone what?"

At that moment, the back doorbell rang. Tally told Greer to wait, suspecting it was her supplier. That's exactly who it was. He carried in a large supply of everything, including the peanuts she had needed the day before.

When Tally returned to her office after signing the forms and sticking a few of the supplies away, Greer was gone from her office. Tally could hear her voice. She was working in the front of the store.

Chapter 19

It was lunchtime before Tally got a chance to finish her interrupted talk with Greer. She gave Greer the first lunch break, telling her to take her sack lunch into the office.

After Tally sat at the desk, she took a moment to regroup her thoughts. She really didn't want to confront Greer, but she had to. "Greer, you'll have to explain this to me. Is there a good reason for you to have a falsified license?"

"Yes, there is. A really good reason." She took a breath, then a bite of the sandwich in her lap, then continued. "My mom and me had to escape. From my father. He was beating us up. We had to change our name."

So her father wasn't dead, either. "Was that at the order of the court?"

"The court? No, there wasn't time for any of that. We just had to get away." She gulped down more of her sandwich and took a swig of her canned soda.

"So you just took off and changed your names? And your father never found you?"

"Nope." She shook her head forcefully. "No, we got away. Clean away. Can I go back to work now?"

She had finished her sandwich.

Tally nodded, but sat for a few more minutes to evaluate what Greer had just told her.

On one hand, it made sense to flee an abusive spouse and parent as quickly as possible. It also made sense to flee secretly, in the middle of the night, so to speak. And her mother was in bad shape. Was that because of having been beaten many times?

On the other hand, why not go through the courts and get the matter taken care of?

Tally read through Greer's paperwork one more time and Greer's story crumbled to bits. She had put down the length of time at her present address as twenty-eight years. Her age was also twenty-eight. Her stories didn't match. She hadn't fled and come to that place.

Or was her license faked to give herself a different age? Had she lied on her job application? In that case, her stories might match. But why wouldn't she admit to that?

Tally went to tell Lily to take her lunch break and decided to skip lunch herself.

* * * *

Yolanda had just delivered a basket to an apartment house where a newlywed wife was going to surprise her husband that night to celebrate their first month of marriage. She was proud of what she'd put together. The sturdy wicker basket held a romantic CD, some scented candles, some of Tally's fudge, and a skimpy nightgown the bride had furnished. Yolanda had also added a few roses and scattered rose petals over everything to remind them of their walk down the aisle.

She wondered, wistfully, if she would ever be preparing gifts for the wedding of her sister and Eden. A beautiful, public marriage, with both sides of the family beaming at the happy couple. Oh, well, she could dream.

Driving past the police station on her way back, she did a double take when she saw Len Abraham being escorted into the station by Detective Jackson Rogers. Len wasn't in handcuffs, but Rogers held him by his upper arm and pulled him along, none too gently.

Oh, good, she thought. They have another suspect.

She called Tally from inside her car as soon as she returned to her parking space behind her shop. "Guess who I just saw?"

"Um, Godzilla? He's attacking Fredericksburg? No, wait, I know. It was probably Batman and Robin. Hallelujah, we're safe."

"Be serious, Tally."

"Then stop making me guess what I can't guess."

Yolanda smiled. Tally had a point. It was so good to have a friend you could be goofy with. She was so glad Tally was back in Fredericksburg. "It was Len," she said. "He was going into the police station."

"Okay."

"That detective had him by the arm. I think he's the next suspect."

"It's about time!" Yolanda heard the smile in Tally's voice.

"I know. He should have been the first suspect, right? The husband is always the first one they look at—in movies and books."

"I wonder if that's what's really going on. Maybe he's getting some of Fran's property or something."

"Her property?" Yolanda said.

"I suppose they processed her clothes, whatever she was wearing."

The sun was beating into Yolanda's car, making it uncomfortably warm with the engine and the AC turned off. "Don't they keep that stuff for a long time?"

"You're right. I hope with all my heart that Dad is off the hook, but I'm afraid to let myself think that," Tally said.

After she finished talking to Tally, Yolanda called Raul, who assured her the shop was doing fine. Not that fine, she thought. If she wasn't needed, that meant there weren't too many customers for him to wait on by himself. She might as well run over and see Kevin. She would drop into his wine store and surprise him.

She left her little Nissan in the parking space behind her own shop, then came around and entered Bear Mountain Vineyards in the front. Kevin wasn't visible, so she peeked down several of the aisles until she saw him, standing with his back to her at the far end of one, talking on his phone.

With a smile, she crept up behind him.

"No, babe. You know I'll always do whatever you want. It's just that—"

No, *babe*? Yolanda halted and listened.

"I always have, lover, I always will. But—" He paused to listen.

Yolanda finished his sentence in her head. "*Always will...lover?*" Ice entered her veins and froze her to the spot, unable to move, almost unable to breathe.

"I know, I know. We need to talk. When can I see you?" Another pause.

"Absolutely. Whenever you want. Let me know, babe."

He quit the call and stuffed the phone into his pocket. When he turned, the shock on his face nearly matched that on hers.

Yolanda wanted to say, "Who will you always love?" but she couldn't speak.

"Yolanda." Kevin's smile was more of a grimace. "Did you just get here?"

Was he hoping she hadn't heard any of his conversation?

"Just now," she managed to say, barely above a whisper. "I...thought I'd drop in and surprise you."

"Yes. You did."

An awkward silence blossomed between them until an older man approached Kevin and asked for help selecting a wine for his shrimp boil.

Yolanda fled before her tears could tumble down her cheeks in front of him.

* * * *

After Tally finished the call with Yolanda about Len being taken into the police station, she broke into a big grin. She couldn't wait to tell her parents tonight.

"What's so great?" Lily asked.

"Huh?"

"You're smiling like you just won the lottery." Lily mirrored Tally's grin.

Maybe her family had won it. "Yeah. It's good news. I'm not sure, but I think they're finally questioning Len."

"About time," Lily said. "Everyone knows he wanted her gone."

"What?"

The store had been empty, but a family of four entered and Tally pulled Lily to the corner.

"What does everyone know?" Tally whispered.

"He's slept around for years and told a bunch of women that he wanted to leave Fran, but he couldn't because they had a prenup and he couldn't afford the divorce."

Tally shook her head. "I heard that. But he could have saved money by not wining and dining other women."

"Those two had the strangest relationship. Fran didn't seem to like Len and he was public about not liking her. But she was jealous anyway."

"Of Shiny, you mean?"

"Of everyone."

"Who else?"

"Me, for one."

"Fran was jealous of you? What did you do?"

Lily gave a *pfft* from the corner of her mouth. "I didn't do anything except show up. I was just interested in dancing. Len latches onto every new female and I was the latest at the time."

"And you caught his roving eye?"

"Yes, he started hanging around me and sort of pestering me."

"Was he harassing you?"

"I guess." Lily shrugged. "He started bringing me flowers and making sure I had whatever I wanted to drink. Which was water. But he kept offering *other* things. I tried to ignore him, but he and Fran were in charge." She screwed her delicate mouth to the side.

"And Fran was jealous, I assume."

"Was she ever! At the cast party after one of the shows, she grabbed me and took me outside, practically threw me to the ground, and told me to never come back to the theater."

"That's...pretty violent."

Lily tossed her head and smiled. "I'm glad she's gone. Now I can dance in the musical productions again."

Chapter 20

"Sh!" Tally hissed. "Not so loud." She glanced around her salesroom and dropped her whisper lower. "Those customers looked at you when you said you're glad Fran is gone."

Lily frowned, but kept her voice down. "Well, I am."

"We all are, but it's not a good thing to say out loud in public." Tally knew Lily was young, but she was smart. She had good potential. She didn't want her making horrible mistakes right now.

Lily regained her usual smile and, with a lightness in her step, crossed the floor to help the family of four who were standing by one of the tables heaped with baked treats.

The rest of the day sped by in a blur of candy making, candy selling, and cleanup toward the end of the day.

When Tally got home, exhausted from the busy day, she sank onto the couch and switched on the afternoon news she had recorded. Nigel immediately jumped up beside her onto the couch cushions with a *thunk*, and started pawing her arm with his velvet touch.

"I know. I need to feed you." Tally hoisted herself up, half paying attention to the news. She made her way into the kitchen and scooped kibble into Nigel's food bowl, then freshened his water. He turned his big eyes up at her. Tally thought he was expressing gratitude, if cats did that. Had his breed, Maine coon, been crossed with a puppy somehow?

"You're welcome," she said, smiling at him.

He started crunching his meal. He made it sound delicious, she thought, as she smiled down on him.

The news announcer's voice drifted in from the living room. "...arrest is based on forensic evidence, the police chief said. What that evidence is, was not disclosed."

Tally whipped into the living room in time to see Len Abraham, handcuffed, being taken into the jail. A sweatshirt was pulled over his head, but the cameraman managed to get a shot of Len's face, alternately scowling and sneering. The coverage of that story seemed to be over.

Tally dialed Jackson's cell number, not knowing if he would answer or not.

"Tally?" Yes, he was taking her call. That was a good sign.

"Is my dad off the hook?"

"No one is off the hook."

"But you just arrested Len."

"That was a couple of hours ago. But yes, we did detain him."

"He's still in jail?"

"For now. He's refusing to talk to us until a lawyer gets here."

So was her dad off the hook or not? "What's the forensic evidence? Can you tell me that?"

"The chief is going to do a press conference at ten. I can't tell you anything before that."

"Thanks, Jackson. At least there's hope."

His voice grew low and grave. "Tally, this isn't over. Don't open the champagne yet."

Still, when she finished the call, her whole body felt lighter, floaty.

She noticed she had a text from Allen. Curious, she opened it. He was telling her he would be back in town tomorrow! She felt even lighter now. She had to tell her mom and dad all about this.

When she went to see her parents a bit later, she breezed into their hotel room. "Did you hear?" she chirped.

"We did," her mother said from the bed, where she lay propped up with a pile of pillows. "Len is being questioned. That's what the news report said."

"I wonder why they pulled him in now," Tally's dad said. "They didn't go after him at first, so why now?"

"I heard the phrase *forensic evidence* on TV," Tally said.

"Fingerprints or DNA, I suppose," Nancy said, weariness in her voice.

Tally took a seat in the chair and set her purse on the floor. Her mother, in spite of acting weary, looked better. "Mom, your color is good. Do you feel better?"

"I do." Nancy sounded surprised when she said it. "I think I'm on the mend."

Bob hovered over her, punching the pillows. "It looks like we'll be able to get out of here on time for our next gig," he said to Tally.

She didn't say anything, but thought, *If the police let you leave.*

"By the way, I called Jackson," she said.

"Jackson?" her father asked.

"The detective. He said the chief is going to announce what the evidence is on the ten o'clock news."

"I have time to get dessert," Tally's father said. "Are you hungry, sweetie?" he asked Tally.

"For dessert? Sure."

After he left, Tally asked her mother if she needed anything.

"I'm doing so much better every day. I wanted to go for a walk outside this morning, breathe some real air, but your father thought I should give it one more day."

"Why don't you get up for a while tonight? Right now? I can help you."

Tally wasn't very big, but her mother wasn't, either. And she wasn't an invalid. She had the strong legs of a dancer, after all.

"Yes, I'll do that."

"It will be good to go gradually, right? A little bit tonight before you try for a longer period tomorrow." Tally stood beside the bed while her mother swung her legs onto the floor and sat up.

"Whoa!" Nancy reeled back.

Tally caught her arm. "Dizzy?"

"I'll say."

Tally put her hand behind her mother's shoulder to support her. "Go slow. Sit for a minute."

Nancy took her time getting up from the edge of the bed. "I have been using the restroom, you know. But I want to walk around a little now and then sit in an actual chair."

It was too bad the room only had one. Tally and Nancy opened the outside door and stepped onto the balcony. A gust of wind caught Nancy's robe and she clutched it tight to her body. They watched traffic go past for a few minutes, then spied Bob's rental car returning.

"Look at you," he said, mounting the steps and walking toward them on the balcony with a white box held in both hands.

"What did you get?" Tally asked.

"Cheesecake. Cherry cheesecake."

Tally knew it was her mom's favorite. They took it inside and each devoured a piece off the paper plates with the plastic forks that Bob had picked up a few days ago.

"Oh look," Nancy said. "It's ten."

Bob switched on the small television that sat on the dresser, as the broadcaster was announcing an upcoming important report on progress in the Frances Abraham case.

"The Frances Abraham case," Bob repeated. "Poor Fran. Get on with it," he said to the TV.

The picture soon displayed the police chief, standing behind a podium that sprouted microphones.

"We have made an arrest today in the Frances Abraham case, based on new forensic evidence."

Yes, Tally thought, I already knew that. Tell us what it is.

"A piece of evidence revealed a new set of fingerprints upon further processing. Leonard Abraham was detained for questioning and is now being held without bail, pending investigation."

A reporter shouted out, "Is he the killer?"

Another one yelled, "Do you have the right person now?"

A few more called out similar things.

The police chief, unflustered, remained silent until they finished and grew quiet. Then he proceeded.

"At this time, we believe we may have the killer in custody. If new details come to light, we will announce them at that time. For now, we're concentrating on Mr. Abraham and believe, as I said, I repeat, that we may have the killer in custody."

He turned abruptly and left with the reporters shouting more questions at his departing back.

"Fingerprints, huh?" Bob said. "I wonder why they think that makes a difference. Mine were on the platter. If his are, too, so what?" He had been sitting beside Tally on the bed and now got up and started pacing.

"It must be more than that, Bob," Nancy said.

He paced faster. "You know what, poppet? I'm going to take a walk."

After he left, Tally's mother said, "I don't think he feels they have any better evidence on Len than they had on him."

"I wish we knew more. Jackson said there would be more details. There were, but barely. He didn't really tell us anything."

"Dear, I think I want to lie down now."

Tally took her mother's arm while she walked to the bed. "You look pale." She wasn't only pale, she was blinking back tears. "Mom, what's the matter?"

Her mother reached for a tissue on the nightstand and dabbed her eyes. "It's Len. He didn't kill Fran. Poor Len. I wish I could go to the jail and see him."

"Mom! Why do you want to do that? You don't know he didn't kill her."

"He's not like that." She looked up at Tally, her blue eyes wide.

Tally thought her mother's eyes might be getting bluer as she grew older. They had always been striking. Now they looked pale and also sorrowful. Why was her mother so upset about Len? She seemed more upset about his arrest than she had been about Fran's death. Did she have…feelings for Len? "Is there something you're not telling me? About Len? And you?"

"Tally, you can see right through me, can't you?" Nancy gave a rueful smile. "The four of us were very close once upon a time. Very close. Yes, Len and I had a…thing. It didn't last long, but I've always held onto fond memories of that time. He was a sweet, gentle, considerate—"

"I get it, Mom." She had to stop her before she said the word *lover.* Tally didn't want to picture her mother having a lover. "Anyway, if all they have is fingerprints, they can't have much. That's all they had on Dad. They'll have to let Len go." Unless, Tally added to herself, he confessed.

She made sure her mother was comfortable, then waited as she fell asleep. When her father returned, she kissed him good-bye on the evening stubble of his cheek and left for her own house. She didn't think, until later, that she never mentioned the fact that Allen would be back in town the next day. But maybe she shouldn't, anyway. She wasn't exactly sure about that relationship and didn't know if she would ever be in the future. No sense telling people about something that didn't exist.

Chapter 21

"What do you think, Nigel?" Tally looked into his deep, round blue eyes, lit by the table lamp beside her bed as she readied herself for the night. They almost looked like smaller versions of her mother's vivid baby blues. Was he trying to understand her? Or was he concentrating on his own thoughts? "Do you think Len could kill his own wife?"

Nigel broke his gaze and swiveled his neck an impossible number of degrees to lick his back.

"Yeah, I don't think he could, either. But why are they holding him? Didn't they learn with Dad that fingerprints aren't enough? They must have more to go on than that. How am I going to find out what it is?"

Lily and Molly were scheduled to work in the morning, Tuesday. Tally cast about for more suspects until very late at night, tossing and turning and annoying Nigel no end.

Before the shop opened, as she watched Molly working, helping stock the display cases in preparation for opening, she asked herself how much she really knew about her. She remembered, from her recent review of the applications, that Molly lived with her parents. Parents, plural. So her father was probably not Wendell. Unless her present dad was a stepdad?

She had yet to try to dig further into Molly's life, as she had the other two, for evidence that she was involved in the past tragedy surrounding Tally's parents today. At the job interview she remembered Molly saying she had dropped out of college to come home due to a "family situation." She hadn't elaborated. Maybe Tally wasn't a good boss for not finding out what the situation was. She would remedy that right now.

"Molly, before we open, can I ask you a couple of questions?"

"Sure." Molly picked up the tray she had just emptied and came to where Tally stood, near the kitchen door. She was eager, Tally knew, and friendly, but had such poor judgment.

"I feel bad that I haven't asked after your family. I know that something necessitated your dropping out of college and I'd like to check, now that you've worked here for a while. Is this job right for you? Is it helping out with your situation?"

"Oh, yes, tons." Molly, much shorter than Tally, looked up at her with a wide smile. "Mom might be ready to go back to work in a month or so, but in the meantime, this extra income has been a lifesaver."

"Is your mother okay?"

"They think she will be. Her chemo will be over in a few weeks and, so far, it looks like it's working."

"She has cancer?"

"Didn't I tell you? Yes, she had both breasts removed. Real bummer. But they keep saying they think they got it all."

Yes, Tally was a bad boss. She should know something this major about her employee. She felt awful for not being aware that Molly's mother had cancer. "I'm very happy to hear that."

"Yeah, thanks. I just wish my dad could go back to work."

"Does he have cancer, too?"

"No, he has this bad back. He's on disability and everything. He probably can't ever work again."

"What did he do?" She should have found this out, too.

"Auto mechanic. That's how I met Howie. He worked with my dad before the accident."

"Howie?"

"We're dating. He picks me up sometimes from here."

Yes, she had mentioned him once before, Tally remembered. She herself had met Howie and remembered him as a strong, compact, short guy with dark hair and a talent for fixing cars. Tally recalled one more thing Molly had said in her interview, that she had dropped out of college to help out the family. "Do you plan on going back to college when your mom starts back to work?"

Molly frowned, looking down. "I don't really know. I've tried to talk to Mom about it, but she doesn't answer me."

"Maybe it would be better to have both incomes?" Tally didn't know how she felt about that. Molly wasn't the best employee in the world, but she would have trouble letting her go, mostly because she hated firing people. She hadn't been able to fire Greer without rehiring her, after all.

If Molly left on her own, though…well, Tally would have to go through that grueling interview process again.

Molly shrugged and went back to getting the shop ready to open.

There was no reason to think that Molly's parents were not her original, biological pair. She couldn't really ask Molly if she had another father who had spent time in prison. She would draw a mental line, for now, through Molly being related to Wendell.

At noon a text pinged to her phone from Allen, asking her to meet him for dinner after she closed up. She replied that she would be there. After she sent the message, she realized she might have to be with her parents. She pushed it out of her mind.

That evening, right after she fed Nigel, Mrs. Gerg came by to collect the rent. Tally had lost track, realizing that she had paid rent on the fifteenth the previous two months.

"I'm so sorry, Mrs. Gerg," she said, getting her checkbook out of her purse. Mrs. Gerg liked to be paid by check.

"Don't think a thing of it, dear." Mrs. Gerg opened her own purse and started searching. Tally knew what that meant. "I've been so busy myself. I had two young couples move into two of my other rentals last week. What a time! All the cleaning and arranging. And paperwork. Oh, my." Her hand emerged triumphant from her bag. "Here it is!" She held out a massive pile of gold chunks.

Tally took it, shook it out slightly, and dangled it from her fingertips. Yes, it was another necklace. This one was so bulky Tally wondered if she would be able to wear a coat over it. "Thank you so much, Mrs. Gerg. It's…very shiny."

She wrote the check and Mrs. Gerg left after Nigel gave her legs a rub and she reciprocated by giving his head the same.

When she went to see her parents, they ordered in pizza and talked about their day while they devoured it.

Tally told them about the new necklace from Mrs. Gerg, then about a young woman in the shop today who had never heard of any of her products, even Twinkies. After she got started, she had enjoyed showing her each and every one and telling her about them. It was extra-fun when the young woman ended up buying an armful.

"How are you two doing?" Tally asked.

"You mother is so much better," her dad said. "We went outside and walked around the parking lot twice."

"Dad, you could take her to a park. It would be prettier."

"That's okay, dear," her mother said, reaching from her perch on the bed to pat Tally's knee where she sat on the desk chair, pulled up to the side of the bed. "It was my idea to walk here. Maybe tomorrow I'll go somewhere else. I do feel, finally, like I'm firmly on the mend." She fished another slice of pizza from the box on the bed between her and Bob and bit off the corner. "We need to get on the road very soon."

"They're waiting for us in Singapore," her dad said. "They were able to book another act for a week, but they want us there soon."

"Does Detective Rogers say you can leave?" Tally asked.

"Well, no, not yet," her mother answered. "But it will have to be soon."

Tally wasn't so sure about that.

Her father excused himself to use the bathroom and Tally took what she told herself was her last slice.

Her mother finished her piece and wiped her hands on one of the napkins that had come with the pizza. "It wore me out being up so much, but it felt so good. Maybe I should take some Tylenol now. Could you get it?"

"In Dad's man purse?"

"Don't call it that where he can hear you."

Tally laughed. "No, I won't." She sat her dad's satchel on the desk and pawed through it.

"Why don't you keep medicines out where you can get them?" she asked her mom.

"I don't know. I think your dad likes to be packed all of the time. We're on the road so much, it's habit for him."

Tally kept digging, not finding the Tylenol. She started taking things out and laying them on the desk. There were programs from their last several shows, lots of loose mints and cough drops, tissues that she hoped were not used, and—another note? She drew it out and read it silently.

I'm not kidding. Pay up or everyone will know who you slept with.

Tally froze, except for her hand, which shook with fear, rattling the paper back and forth.

"Tally? What is it?"

Her mother got up from her seat on the bed and came over to her. "What are you holding?"

"What is this, Mom?" She held the note out and Nancy took it.

"Oh dear," she said, stumbling back to the bed and sinking onto it.

"This isn't an old note from years ago," Tally said. "It's new."

"Yes, it is."

"What's it about? Who is it to? Have you seen this before?"

Nancy hung her head. "No. But I think I know what it is."

Chapter 22

Tally's father returned from the bathroom and they both stared at him. Tally supposed they looked guilty because he said, "What's wrong? What have you done? Tally? Are you snooping in my things?"

"Bob, she was getting a pain pill for me." Nancy stepped toward him, shielding Tally.

Tally picked up the paper that her mother had dropped beside her on the bedcover. She could have stuffed it back into the satchel, but she had to know what it was about. She thrust it toward her father.

"Was this note written to you, Dad?"

"You found it." His voice was flat as he plopped onto the bed beside his wife. "Nancy, my dear poppet, I didn't want you to see it." He looked up at Tally. His eyes were troubled. "Nor you, sweetheart." His shoulders drooped as he blew out a noisy breath.

"Come here." He patted the bed next to him and Tally sat. He put one arm around each woman and hugged both of them tight to his chest.

"I'm being blackmailed. Again. Right now."

"By Wendell?" Tally asked.

"No, not this time. By Len. Your mother knows all about what happened back then. But other people don't. The police don't. We were indiscreet when we were younger. One night we had all been drinking far too much and we traded partners with the Abrahams."

Traded partners? Tally was shocked. She knew her mother had had a fling with Len, but she understood that was before either of them were married. Now her father was telling her they were…swingers?

"Just one time?" Tally asked. Once would be bad enough.

"Just a…few times," her father said, dragging his words out.

"It was no big deal," her mother added, talking quickly. "We all four agreed to keep it to ourselves."

"And we always have," Bob said. "Until now."

"So what's this about?" Tally asked, completely befuddled. "What does something that happened a million years ago have to do with this mess now?"

"I couldn't figure that out, either," Bob said. "But I talked to him. Len thinks that I slept with Fran again. Just the other day."

"Why does he think that?" Tally wondered if it was true. The fact that the doubt was there troubled her and a coldness spread through her whole body.

"Fran started pestering Bob as soon as we got to town," Nancy said. "A few years after we left for the first time, she decided she hated me. All of a sudden. Every time we've come to town, she's made it a point to publicly snub me, or to accuse me of something."

"I think," Bob said, "she thought she could get to Nancy through me this time."

"She always has to just pick at me until I lose my temper with her."

"She somehow found out when we were getting here and was waiting for me when we checked in to the hotel."

"She waylaid Bob at the front desk," Nancy said, "and told him she needed to see him privately. I was already beginning to feel bad, tired. Now I know why. It was from this dengue fever, I'm sure. So I told them to go into the bar and I'd go up to the room with the bellhop."

"We each ordered a drink," Bob said. "When they came, Fran swigged her martini in about three gulps while I had a sip of beer. She started flirting and I shut her down. Then she got nasty. She said she was going to tell Len and Nancy that we had a fling that night. I laughed at her. Probably a mistake."

"But, what was she thinking?" Nancy said. "A fling. Right. For what? Ten minutes? Fifteen minutes? That's all you were together."

"I didn't even finish my beer," he said. "I told her good night and came up to our room."

"So why did Len write this blackmail note?" Tally asked, still as confused as before.

"Len called our room about an hour later," Bob said. "Fran had just then told him we slept together and he believed her. She'd been gone long enough for it, at that point. I don't know where she went after she left here. Now that someone has murdered her, all I can think of is that he thinks this makes me a good suspect."

"That's crazy," Tally said.

Kaye George

"They're both crazy," Nancy said, much too loudly. "I mean *were*. Was." Her voice broke. "She was. He is."

"So this isn't a problem for you, right?" Tally said to her dad.

He looked away for a moment. "It kind of is," he said.

"Why?" Nancy asked. "What did you do?"

"After Fran died, I met him and paid him what he was demanding. I thought it would make it easier for us. I went to their house and gave him some money on the front porch. Now he says he photographed our transaction with their security camera."

* * * *

Yolanda had cried herself out after hearing Kevin on the phone with *babe*, saying he would do whatever she wanted him to. Would he ever say that to her? She ignored his phone calls all last night and today. She was hurt, humiliated, and frankly, embarrassed. How could she have believed they had a thing going? That he cared for her? The memory of his kind eyes, his warm smile, wouldn't leave her alone, though.

Now, at home after a dull day at work with not enough business, she decided she was just plain angry. She picked up her bright pink phone and answered his next call.

"Yolanda? I have to talk to you."

"Okay. Talk."

"No," he said, anguish breaking up his words. "I have to talk to you... in person. I have to tell you...what's going on."

"I think I figured that out." Even to herself, her words sounded angry, cold, and clipped.

"No, you didn't. Can I come in?"

"In? Where are you?" She stepped to her front living room window and peered through the darkness.

"In your front yard."

At first, her yard looked empty. Then she saw him. He was hard to spot because he was, as always, dressed in black. The nearby streetlight threw his shadow onto her sidewalk.

"Please? Can I talk to you?"

She relented and opened her door. They looked at each other awkwardly until Yolanda stepped aside and let him in. She turned her back and sat in the wingback chair so he couldn't sit beside her. He perched on the edge of the cushion of the brocade couch.

"I wanted to bring you flowers," he said, "but you have a shop full. And that's kind of...sappy."

Yolanda clamped her lips shut, not daring to say what was on her mind.

"I haven't been honest with you."

"Oh, you think?" Her words sounded shrill. She should keep her mouth shut, she thought. Just let him try to explain this.

"I'm married and lived with her until a few months ago. We've been going through a divorce for a year and a half."

"And you'll always do whatever she wants you to."

"Right now I will. I've been trying to divorce her for over a year now. I definitely do not want to be married to her. She's devious and manipulative, so I tell her what she wants to hear. If I could do something to make her agree to sign the papers, I would. She's hot and cold on the divorce and I'm getting so tired of it." He cradled his forehead in his hand for a moment. "Nothing will make her agree to any terms that my lawyer sets out."

Yolanda had to admit, she was interested. If what he said was true, it must be awful for him. "What does she want?"

"I wish I knew. She likes for me to be confused, I know that."

"Does she want money?"

"I've offered her an awful lot a couple of different times. She'll say it's fine, then she'll change her mind."

"So you just have to stay married to her?"

"My lawyer says that it's been long enough. I can go before a judge by myself, without her, and get it done."

"By yourself? Really? How does that work?" Yolanda thought people had to go to Reno, or someplace, to do that.

"The laws in Texas let people divorce even when the other one doesn't want to. I have a court date next month."

He did seem serious about the divorce. Yolanda had been thinking she was just another foolish, duped woman who dated a married man. They always said they were getting a divorce. Maybe Kevin really was?

"Where does she live?"

"She moved to Amarillo last year. I keep hoping she'll meet someone else and we can make a clean break. Hasn't happened yet, though."

They both fell silent. Kevin stared at the floor, waiting for Yolanda to speak, having said his piece.

"Kevin, you'll have to give me some time to think about this."

He raised his head and implored her with his eyes. "I'm sorry I never told you. Every week I keep thinking it's almost over. I'm almost rid of her. Then...it falls through. Again."

Yolanda shook her head. "I'll talk to y'all later, okay?"

He gave a slight smile and nodded. "Okay."

After he left, she lay awake in bed, conflicted and confused. It was a lot to deal with. She very much wished that Kevin had told her all of this up front. The past could certainly mess things up in the present. Especially if you tried to bury it.

It was going to take her a while to process it.

Chapter 23

Tally left her parents to comfort each other as best they could and went home. After parking in the driveway, she walked to the front steps, sensing the welcome of the big live oak trees that dotted her front yard. She slowly opened her front door and went into the house, feeling numb. She dropped her purse onto the floor, shoved Nigel over, and sat on the couch. Annoyed, he stared at her until she broke into a smile and petted him.

The iciness inside her remained, though, even as she buried her hands in Nigel's warm, soft fur. Her father had paid a blackmailer. Why would he do that? She couldn't help but think he might have paid him because the accusation was true. He denied it, but it made good sense that the payment might have been necessary. Her head fell back on the couch cushion, she closed her eyes, and hoped her mother wasn't having the same thoughts.

If her dad had slept with Fran that first night and was lying about it, what else could he be lying about? No, she shouted at herself silently. No, no, no. He did not sleep with Fran or kill her.

Nigel thumped down and made tiny noises in his throat while he headed toward his empty food bowl.

"Hey, big guy, I fed you. You ate all of it." Her despair lifted an inch or two as she plucked up her hefty cat and carried him into her bathroom, where she got ready for bed. He crouched on the sink counter, intently following each motion of her bedtime ritual.

She glanced at her phone before getting into bed. Allen had left a text.

Allen! She had forgotten all about him. She had stood him up. It was awfully late now. She'd contact him in the morning.

* * * *

Sleep came hours too late and she awoke groggy and not well rested.

Wednesday at the shop went slow. She texted Allen a couple of times with apologies, but got no response. The whole day seemed to match Tally's doldrums. The sky clouded over most of the day, a rare occurrence for August in those parts.

Tally was doodling on a pad of paper when Lily spoke up. "You need an event."

"An event?"

"Yeah. Maybe... like—I know! Labor Day is coming up. Something for that?"

An event like the one that killed Fran Abraham? That was her first thought. Then she changed her mind. "I think you're right. We do need an event. But not like the last one."

"Why don't you have it at Bella's Baskets? Or Bear Mountain Vineyards?"

"That's an idea. It could mainly be a wine tasting."

"And you can bring your sweets, too."

Tally warmed to the idea. When she shared it with Yolanda, she was in favor, too.

"I like it," Yolanda said on the phone from her shop. "A wine tasting. We should do it at Kevin's. We could both display and sell our wares. I'll call him. I think he'll like it."

Tally hoped Yolanda was right. This could be good for all three of their shops.

After that, the customers were steady, with no rushes, no crowds. It seemed there were fewer sales than usual, but when she counted everything up at the end of the day and took stock of what was left, it hadn't been that bad. The whole day was colored by her sour mood.

And another thing: How long had it been since she had heard from Jackson Rogers? Was it because he was so super-busy on the case? Pursuing lots of other suspects? Other than Fran's husband and her lover? Possible lover? She could hope, but she didn't really believe that. Who else was there?

Len and her dad seemed to be at the top of the list. Tally still felt that a relative of Wendell or Owen might have been exacting revenge, but she couldn't see that the police were pursuing that aspect at all. There were all sorts of others to suspect, even though the police weren't concentrating on them, that she could tell. What about Shiny? And Ionia? They both had cause to hate Fran. They were both better off without her. Shiny, because she was after Fran's husband, even though he didn't stick to one woman on the side for very long. And Ionia wanted Fran's job. How badly? Tally wondered.

When she got to her parents' room that night, she asked her mother.

"How well do you know Ionia?" she asked.

"We're very old friends," Nancy said. "I'm so happy for her. When all the mess is over, she'll be in a good place."

"When?" Tally asked, not following her mother's logic.

"We had lunch."

"You did?" That was good news. "You went out to lunch? Was it okay? Did you tire yourself out?"

"We just went real close to here."

"But she walked there," Bob said. "I went with her to make sure she made it, then left her and Ionia to eat and gab." He gazed fondly at his wife. "You feel strong today, don't you, poppet?"

Nancy nodded. "As soon as we get the go-ahead, I'm ready to leave. I'm ready to go back onto the stage."

Bob raised his eyebrows. "You're not one hundred percent, dear. Let's be gradual."

"Oh, phooey. I'll be all the way back in a day or two more. I can feel it."

"Mom," Tally said, barging into their banter. "What did you and Ionia talk about?"

"Oh, just stuff. You know."

"But you said you were happy for her."

"Oh, yes. I guess no one knows this yet, but she was given Fran's job."

Tally's mouth fell open. "Fran being gone is working out perfectly for her, isn't it?"

Nancy gave a small laugh. "Oh, no, it's not like that. The board gave her the job before Fran was killed. They haven't announced it yet. In fact, they hadn't fired Fran yet."

"When will they announce it?"

"Ionia said they told her 'when the dust settles.'"

"I guess the police will have to catch the killer first, don't you?" Bob asked.

Tally agreed. "I assume the board is waiting for the legal authorities to give them the go-ahead?"

"Oh, yes, they were told not to make anything public until permission is granted," Nancy said.

Tally didn't say it, but she was sure that Jackson would have to be certain Ionia didn't kill Fran before anything would be allowed to be announced.

Soon after she returned home, Lily texted that she wasn't feeling well and asked to have a day off. Tally told her that would be fine, since Molly would be working.

However, Molly called late that night, too, asking if she could have the day off on Thursday.

"Mom is having a bad reaction from her last chemo and I'd like to stay with her tomorrow."

"Of course, Molly. I'm sorry to hear that, but you need to take care of her. I'll call Greer."

"Thanks so much, Miss Tally. I can work Friday. I hope."

"Just let me know, okay?"

She glanced at the clock. It was after 9:30, but maybe that wasn't too late. She got ahold of Greer, who said she could make it to work Thursday.

However, Greer was late again in the morning. "Setting Sun Home called me an hour ago."

"Setting Sun?" Tally had seen a sign with that name on it on a large institutional-looking building on the east side of town.

"The nursing home. Mom is giving them fits. I went over to try to calm her down, but she's acting wild."

Tally saw tears threatening to spill from Greer's eyes. Tally grabbed a tissue from under the counter and handed it to her.

"You and Molly both have a lot going on with your moms, don't you? I thought your mom lived with you."

"She had to go to that home, Setting Sun. She got a lot worse and I couldn't take care of her."

"Is she better now that she's there, being taken care of?"

"Not really. They gave her a shot and knocked her out. I hate when they do that. She's a zombie the rest of the day. And they just let her lie there, they don't pay any attention to her. That's how she gets those bedsores. They let her get so dirty."

"Oh, honey, I'm so sorry it has to be that way." Tally hugged Greer and patted her head, almost dislodging the clip she always wore to keep her unruly hair up.

Even though she was older than all of her employees, Tally's parents were in good shape. She felt so lucky. That is, her mother would be in good shape when she recovered from her bout of dengue fever. At the moment, even under the weather, she was probably stronger and more fit than either of their moms.

"Would you mind if I looked in on your mother sometimes?" Tally said. "Maybe if more people are coming by, they will pay more attention and take better care of her."

Greer stared, her red lips forming a perfect O. "That would be awesome. I mean, you don't have to do that, but…"

"I wouldn't mind. My parents will be leaving town soon and I'll have extra time after they go so I can help you out."

"Yeah. That would be great." Greer swiped at her tears, then her nose with the tissue, and straightened. "We'd better get to work. We should have opened ten minutes ago."

It was more like twenty, but Tally agreed and they both got to work.

At about eleven o'clock, Allen came into the shop. Tally was working in front and saw him immediately. One glance at his face showed Tally he wasn't happy.

"Let's go outside and talk," she said, opening the door and stepping onto the hot sidewalk.

He followed, as she'd hoped he would.

"My parents…I forgot all about dinner. They're having such a hard time."

"Yeah, everyone's having a hard time, aren't they?" He gave her a cold, direct stare.

"Allen, they are tangled up in a murder investigation. They were supposed to do a show tomorrow and the police won't let them leave town."

He looked away. "I can leave town. In fact, I'm thinking of relocating."

Tally blinked. "Relocating? Where? Out of town?"

"That's what I just said, isn't it?"

He waited for an answer, so she shrugged. "I guess."

"I can move to Fort Worth for this job. They have most of their warehouses there. It's like the hub for the company."

Tally remained silent, waiting for him to tell her he was moving.

He looked away. "I haven't decided yet, if I want to go there."

"Do you like the work?"

"It's okay. I don't mind the driving."

"And you like the company, the people?"

He blew out a breath. "Do you want me to move? You don't care?"

"I didn't say that. We just…we don't know each other very well. I want you to…be happy. To do what you like."

"I don't know what I like. I thought I liked you."

He turned and she watched him walk away for half a block, then went back inside the air-conditioning and got to work.

* * * *

Kevin called Yolanda in the early afternoon. She knew she'd been missing him, but was surprised how her body reacted to the sound of his voice.

"Kevin," she said, probably sounding like a teenager. "I'm glad you called."

"Why is that?"

Why did he say that? "Well, I just...I'm glad y'all called. That's all."

"Have you eaten lunch?"

She had just gotten back from a basket delivery and was thinking about sending Raul to get something for both of them. "Not yet. I'm going to in a few minutes."

"I'll treat, if you can leave. I have to go out to the vineyard and pick up a couple cases of wine that are ready for the shop. If you want to come along, we can grab something while we're out."

"Let me check." She was surprised how hard her heart was beating. "Raul," she called. "Have you had lunch?"

"I have," he called from the back of the shop. "I brought mine in today. Just finished it."

"Do we have any more orders to go out today?"

"Just a sec." He was, she knew, consulting the schedule they kept on her desk back there. "Next one is day after tomorrow."

That wasn't good news for her business. But it was for seeing Kevin. He told her to come next door in ten minutes.

Yolanda knew the grin on her face looked foolish. "Raul," she said, going to the area behind the counter to where he was now culling the flowers in the cooler, removing those that were too old to use. "I have to go out for an hour or so. It's slow, so if you want to close up, y'all can just come back tomorrow morning."

"You look happy," he said. "Are you going to see Kevin?"

"Aren't you perceptive?" She chuckled. "As a matter of fact, I am."

"We're getting short on flowers. I could pick up some more carnations this afternoon and bring them back here. I can go home after that."

She had an account at the florist's, so he could get the flowers and they would put them on her charge card. "That's a good idea. See you tomorrow." She hurried out the back door to Kevin's place.

He was locking his back door as she approached. They both climbed into his truck, a white pickup with the Bear Mountain logo on the driver's door. The atmosphere was a bit formal as they started the drive out of town to his vineyard. They started discussing the weather, then Kevin started discussing the wine tasting.

"That was Lily's idea," Yolanda said. "I know Tally thinks she's having trouble finding good help, but at least she has Lily. She's a gem."

"It's a great idea. I think I have the wines all planned. And I've been thinking about the pairings."

"Pairings?"

"Yes, we can pair each wine with one of Tally's sweets."

She caught his excitement as they discussed what would be best with what, rejected some ideas, and came up with new ones.

By the time they got to the turnoff, they were chatting like there had never been any trouble between them. The truck bumped down the dirt and gravel road, past the large sign designating the area as Bear Mountain Vineyards, and rolled to a stop beside one of the buildings on the property.

They both hopped out and Yolanda enjoyed the heat of the sunshine on her upturned face while Kevin unlocked the door of the storage shed. His field workers had left two crates of wine in it for him to pick up. The building where the vine was fermented was at the other end of the vineyard, across the vast fields and rows of gnarled, trellised vines.

Kevin stepped into the darkness and stooped to lift the first crate from the floor. Yolanda couldn't resist. She hugged him from behind.

He abandoned his task and concentrated on exchanging a long overdue kiss with her. Then another. Then another. Eventually, they got the wine loaded into his truck and drove to a drive-through to pick up burgers and fries, which they ate, parked in the shade at the edge of the park.

Yolanda felt her heart singing the rest of the day.

Chapter 24

Tally was surprised to see Shiny Peth come into the shop in the early afternoon saying she wanted some sweets for herself. Even though she had bought an awful lot of candy to celebrate her engagement last week, Tally thought she was the kind of woman who kept an eagle eye on her figure. Vintage sweets were not the ideal snack for someone trying to stay ultrathin.

Heads always turned when Shiny was on the scene and today was no exception. She looked her usual stunning self, apparently completely recovered from the binge she'd been on. Three young local women clustered together on the other side of the room, obviously whispering about her, and at the same time, trying to act like they weren't noticing her.

"Is Lily here?" Shiny asked.

Tally said she wasn't and could she help her.

"Can you tell me anything about these?" Shiny asked Tally. She picked up a box of Clark Bars. "Are there a lot of artificial ingredients?"

It was one of Tally's simpler recipes and she explained what was in them. "It's mostly Rice Krispies, so any preservatives are what's already in them."

"Well, what else are they?"

Her raspy tone sounded belligerent, but Tally answered with her Sales Smile. "Sugar, corn syrup, peanut butter, and chocolate chips. We boil the sugar and syrup together, add the peanut butter, and stir in the cereal. We press that in a flat pan and cover it all with melted chocolate chips."

"What else do you add?"

Shiny still sounded like she was trying to catch her out in a lie, but Tally kept her smile in place. "Nothing. That's it."

Frowning, Shiny stared at the package. "You're sure?"

Tally's smile slipped a bit. "I know what's in my products. We make them all right here in my kitchen."

The tallest of the three women who'd been staring at Shiny was suddenly at Tally's elbow. "I've seen you on the stage," she said, looking starstruck.

"Not recently." Shiny pulled her mouth sideways. "Fran fired me and told me not to come back."

Another of the trio appeared behind the first one. "I know," she said. "You were with Fran's husband one time and I heard you saying you wished Fran was dead."

"I am not seeing Lennie Abraham anymore. I could care less if that woman is dead or alive."

"She died the same night," the woman said.

Shiny's lips tightened as she thrust the package into Tally's hands and fled the store.

That was odd, thought Tally. Why had Shiny come in here? Had she really wanted to buy something? Maybe she'd wanted to talk to Lily. The last time she'd been in the shop she'd been showing off a ring that Lennie had given her. The engagement was off already?

Tally cocked her head to think. She pictured Shiny's hand just now, holding the package of Clark Bars. No, Shiny wasn't wearing that ring anymore. Maybe she and Lennie really were done with each other. It didn't mean Shiny didn't kill Fran. Maybe she did, and that caused guilt and bad tension between her and Lennie and broke them up. The same thing could happen if Lennie killed Fran, too. It was all so confusing.

Greer asked to leave early to check on her mother. The shop was busy and Tally would rather she stayed to help out, but after their conversation this morning about how badly the nursing home was treating her mom, Tally let her go.

Tally had planned, after their talk earlier, to drop in and visit Greer's mother after work, but she was so worn out from toiling alone for the last two hours, that she went home and snuggled with Nigel.

The next day, Tally was happy to see Lily come to work.

"I hope you're feeling better," Tally said. She couldn't let Lily work if she was still sick, for the protection of her customers.

"Completely over it. I ate some yogurt that was too old, I think. My tummy was upset until about two in the morning. I'll spare you the details."

Tally was glad of that.

"I'm tired today, but I ate a good breakfast, I was so hungry. Don't worry, I threw the rest of that batch of yogurt out. On the way home tonight I'll get some more."

Lily stood there for a moment.

"Is there something else?" Tally asked.

Lily pulled three sheets of paper from her pocket and smoothed them onto the top of the glass candy case. "I made some posters for the wine tasting. Which one do you like best?"

Tally stared at them in amazement. "These are terrific. Really. They're very good."

"Well, I do want to go into advertising. I've been studying it a little."

"Did you do these while you were sick?"

"I started feeling better last night and I was bored."

One was framed with plump bunches of grapes and done in blues and purples, with bright yellow lettering, much like the web page. The second one showed the front of Bear Mountain Vineyards with a lot of brown tones, and the third displayed rows of gleaming wine bottles. It was maybe too dark.

Tally had a hard time choosing, but picked the one that looked the most like the web page Lily had designed. "This one, I think. What do you want to do with it?"

"Could I get some made? At the printshop? I'll put them up myself."

"Where? Around Fredericksburg, I guess?"

"Yes, in other shops and the library, on phone poles, places like that."

"Lily, you're a genius." She wanted to hug her, but patted her shoulder instead. Maybe hugging was too personal between boss and employee.

Lily picked up the papers and stuffed them back into her pocket. "The thing is...well... could you pay for them?"

"Yes, of course. How much do you think it will be?" Tally hoped the cost wouldn't be too high.

The figure Lily named was doable. She had already researched that aspect, too.

"Go for it, Lily. This will be great. Have the printshop call me to get my credit card number, okay?"

"That'll be fine." Lily went to work with a smile on her face.

Molly was also able to make it in, to Tally's relief. It was good to have adequate help in the shop. Friday was usually a busy day, leading into the weekend.

"Is your mom better today?" she asked Molly.

"Much better. She didn't get up off the couch hardly at all yesterday, just to go to the bathroom. I brought her meals, but she couldn't eat much. She felt so much better that she got up and fixed breakfast today."

"I'm so glad to hear that." It was a good breakfast day all around. Tally had even eaten more than usual, a bowl of oatmeal with raisins and brown sugar.

* * * *

Yolanda wandered aimlessly around her shop, picking up a basket, then setting it down. Picking up some ribbon and moving it six inches. Opening the flower cooler, staring at the flowers, then shutting the door.

"What's bothering you?" Raul asked.

"Oh, nothing," she said, not wanting to talk about Kevin with him.

"It's a pretty big nothing." He gave her a look that might have held some pity.

She was feeling pitiful. Why had she kissed Kevin in the shed? Could she trust him? She really didn't know. His story sounded good, but was it true? Did she know anything about him for sure? Only that she loved him. Did he love her? Was she a tramp, seeing a semi-married man?

"Nothing's happening, Raul," she said. "Let's close up early."

She needed to go home and decide what to do. Somehow.

* * * *

Since Tally had been tied down on Thursday, she needed to squeeze in a grocery store run some time today. She called ahead for curbside pickup and when there was a midmorning lull, she dashed out. She drove to the grocery store and pulled around for the pickup.

On the way back, she took an alternate route past the county park, enjoying the pleasant weather. It wasn't blistering hot and a steady breeze brought the scent of the lavender fields from outside town into Fredericksburg. She slowed when she saw a familiar figure, wild brown hair clipped up on top of her head. Greer was sitting on a bench, smoking. That was none of her business since it was nowhere near her shop, but the man sitting beside her looked much too old for her. Tally wondered if Greer was involved with someone she shouldn't be. Greer wasn't looking in her direction, so she was able to gawk and get a good look at her smoking companion. They were both vaping, she noted. The guy was rough-looking, unshaven, but not in a cool, sexy-stubble sort of way, and had a ragged haircut. He wore that kind of sleeveless undershirt that looked like a tank top, and his bare arms were covered with dark tattoos, the kind she thought of as prison tats.

Tally drove the rest of the way trying to think of a way to bring up the subject of inappropriate companions with Greer when she came to work Saturday, tomorrow. She had to be subtle about it, since it really wasn't any of her business.

As she was finishing loading the flour and sugar into the cupboard, she heard Shiny's unmistakable annoying voice out front. Tally assumed Shiny had returned to talk to Lily, since she hadn't been able to yesterday. Slightly alarmed at Shiny's volume and her angry tone, she rushed to the salesroom to find Lily backed up against the glass display case, Shiny leaning into her in a threatening manner.

"You stay away from Randy, you hear me?" Shiny wasn't quite shouting, but she was awfully loud.

"Shiny, back up and get away from Lily." Tally used the most commanding voice she could, one degree louder than Shiny's. "Leave her alone. What's the matter with you?" When Shiny didn't move, Tally tugged at Shiny's shoulder and pulled her back a step. Lily moved out of range, her brown eyes open wide in fright.

"Are you okay?" Tally asked Lily, keeping her hand on Shiny.

"She needs to stay away from Randy," Shiny repeated, and shrugged Tally off her.

Lily stuck her lower jaw out and answered. "I'll buy shoes from him whenever I want." Lily walked across the room and out of range, frowning.

"Shiny, you cannot come in here and harass my help," Tally said.

"And she can't steal my boyfriend."

Tally wasn't feeling charitable toward Shiny at the moment, so she said, "Is that the guy who was propping you up when you were so drunk a week ago?"

"Randy's a very nice guy. I don't want Lily making a play for him. I hope that's clear now."

"I don't want your old boyfriend. He's no prize," Lily called from the other side of the shop, obviously not in a charitable mood, either. "Next time I buy ballet shoes, I'll buy them at his shop again. He's the only one in town who sells them."

Shiny threw an ugly look at Lily and stormed out of the store.

It took the atmosphere ten or fifteen minutes to calm down and for the customers to quit buzzing and get back to buying.

Chapter 25

Lily swept the front room while Molly and Tally tidied the kitchen after closing, then Tally locked up and they all headed out.

Tally had asked Lily for a copy of the poster they'd chosen because she wanted to show it to Yolanda. Lily had it saved online and was able to print one out in the office, so Tally saw Lily and Molly out the back and she went out the front, heading for Bella's Baskets. Greer was walking toward her and stopped when she saw Tally.

"Greer, was that you I saw you in the park yesterday?" she began.

Greer stopped walking and stared at Tally. "In the park? The park? I don't think so."

"It's okay. I don't care if you smoke when you're not at work."

"I wasn't there. It wasn't me." She whirled, changing her direction, and stalked away. The nursing home was in that direction and Tally wondered if she was going there.

Yolanda and Raul were both gone and Bella's Baskets was locked, so Tally went home, musing on her way. So much for playing Big Sister and handing out her sage advice to Greer. She'd try to think of another way to approach this. Maybe she'd see them together again. Or maybe not, which would be good. She would be sure to remember what the scruffy, older man looked like in case she saw him with Greer again. If that happened, Tally wouldn't accept Greer's denial that she was with him.

After she got home, she talked things out with Nigel.

"I have to figure Greer out," she said.

Nigel blinked and cleaned his whiskers with a paw, having just polished off his din-din.

"She was obviously with this much older man. Why would she deny it?"

Nigel ignored that remark as being beneath him.

"Yeah, you're right. I'd deny it, too, if I were dating someone like that. My mother would have a fit."

An ear twitch told her to continue that line of thought.

"Oh, what about this? What about *her* mother? I wonder if *she* would approve?"

The cat's direct stare made Tally think harder. "Aha. I said I would visit her mother, right? To see if she's being taken care of. I think it would be best if I filled in for the times Greer can't be there, but for this visit... well, I think I'll just go and see what's what. If Greer is there, we can both visit her mother."

She had seen her parents almost every night and she thought she could take a night off. A brief call assured her that they were doing well, her mother feeling more and more healthy and her dad sounding optimistic.

Greer had mentioned the name of the home, Setting Sun, which wasn't far. The air had cooled off after dark and Tally decided to walk. As she came in the front door of the place, Greer was at a counter in the small lobby, writing. She must have been on her way here when they met on the sidewalk.

"Greer," she called. "I came to see your mom. I'm glad you're here."

"Oh. Tally." Greer seemed surprised to see her, but smiled. "You have to sign in here."

"Sure." Tally came forward.

"Wait, I'll sign you in." Greer scribbled Tally's name and the time in the book and led the way down a dim hallway.

The lobby had held a faint distasteful smell, but the hallway reeked. It was, Tally decided, a mixture of odors, but predominantly the sharp, pungent tang of urine. They passed doorways to small rooms. Tally peeked into them, finding some empty and some holding bedridden skeletal beings who were either on IVs, or propped up in their hospital beds watching television, or lying flat and looking, to Tally, like they were already dead.

She tried to breathe shallowly to avoid the smells.

The end of the hallway opened to a common room where wheelchairs were lined up in front of a loud television, tuned to a movie channel. Those not in wheelchairs were propped with pillows in plastic-covered armchairs. Two or three of the eighteen or twenty oldsters watched the television, some gazed ahead vacantly, and one picked at her bathrobe with one hand, muttering something too softly for Tally to hear.

Greer went over to the woman plucking her clothing. She was so thin that two pillows were needed, one on each side of her, to hold her straight in the wheelchair.

"Mom, I'm here," Greer said, putting her face in front of the woman and stilling her restless hand, holding it in her own. "Are you having a good day?"

This was the woman Tally had seen in the wheelchair outside the apartment when she'd surreptitiously driven by on Sunday.

Greer's mother turned her head with agonizing slowness, her mouth agape and her muttering silenced. When she caught sight of her daughter, an angelic smile transformed her haggard look. But only on one side of her face. They other side drooped. Tally noticed again that one arm was held bent against her body. The woman had definitely had a stroke.

"Greer. Darling. I haven't seen you in so long." Her speech was a bit slurred, but understandable.

Greer gave Tally a side glance and whispered that her mother never remembered her coming to see her. She must have dementia, too, Tally thought.

"It's so good of you to come. Can I get you something?" Greer's mother looked around, maybe to see if there was something she could serve to her daughter. "Who's this?" she asked when she saw Tally.

"This is Tally Holt, Mom, my new boss. I work for her."

"How nice. I'm glad you have a job, dear." Her smile dissolved into a worried look. "Have you seen your father? I can't seem to locate him. He's gone off again."

"He's doing fine, Mom. I saw him today."

"Next time you see him, tell him I forgive him. He can come home now."

Greer bit her lower lip, then smiled at her mother and patted her bony hand. "I will, Mom. I'll tell him."

* * * *

Later, at home, Greer's statement came back to Tally as she was falling asleep. It jerked her wide-awake. Greer told her mother she had seen her father that day. At the time, Tally assumed Greer was placating her mother by lying. Reassuring her so she wouldn't get agitated. But what if she *had* seen him? What if the man in the park vaping with her was her father?

The man had looked one step from homeless. Or maybe he *was* homeless. Greer lived in a dilapidated apartment building. Her mother, a stroke victim who seemed to have dementia, was now in a miserable nursing home, presumably on Medicaid. Tally fell asleep worrying about Greer's family situation.

It was still on her mind in the morning when Greer came into work—on time, she was happy to see. Tally brought it up before they opened and got busy and before she could forget.

"Greer, was that your father I saw you with yesterday?"

"Yesterday? Where?" She kept her head down, getting sweets from the refrigerator and putting them on a tray.

"In the park. You were both on a bench, doing that vaping thing."

"No. I wasn't. No. That wasn't my father. He doesn't live around here. And I wasn't there." She lifted the tray of candies and hurried past Tally to go to the front and put them out for sale.

Tally pursed her lips. She couldn't help but be angry that Greer kept lying to her. How did she think Tally would believe what she said, when she had seen them? Something was off about Greer.

She got a call at about one o'clock in the afternoon from her mother.

"They've brought your dad in to the police station again." She was breathless, panting. "I don't know what to do. I think it's all my fault."

Tally was more than breathless. She was speechless.

"What do you mean? How is this your fault?"

"They asked me some questions and I think I...said the wrong thing. They have new information, they said."

"What did you say?"

"I—I'm not sure. Can you go down there to the station? Can you find out what's going on from that detective?"

"I don't know, but I'll try." This had to stop. It was bordering on harassment of her parents. What was Detective Rogers doing?

She told Lily and Greer that she had a family emergency and left them abruptly without answering the questions they called out to her departing back.

Chapter 26

Tally fumed all the way to the police station. When she reached it, she sat in her car for a few moments to collect herself. She wouldn't get anywhere with Jackson Rogers if she stormed into the station all hot and bothered. After some deep breaths, she gathered her wits and made herself walk slowly into the lobby and ask for Detective Rogers.

Although she had asked for him, it surprised her that he came out to see her at all, let alone to the lobby. He wasn't holed up in a small, cramped room, badgering her father with ridiculous questions.

She stood almost toe to toe with him, looking up because he was quite a bit taller, after all. "Why are you holding my dad? You know he didn't kill Fran."

Rogers took a step back. "I don't know anything for sure at this point."

"Do you even know how she was killed?"

"We don't have the tox back yet, but it should be here soon. There's a rush on it."

"How can you arrest him when you don't know how she was killed?"

He looked her in the eye, then looked away.

"What did my mother say? She thinks she said something."

"She's been cooperating."

"Can I see my dad?"

"Not right now. He'll call you or your mother when he's available. Please, Tally, go home and let us do this. We need to figure it all out."

"But you do have new information, right? What is it?"

He turned his back on her and left the lobby.

Tally drove straight over to see her mother.

"They just kept asking me and asking me," she said.

"About?"

"Those blackmail notes. They found them."

"They're old, right? Years old." Except that new one. "Did Len tell them about the new one?"

"No, I did. I didn't mean to. I let it slip."

"Let me get all this straight, Mom. Dad met Fran for a drink. In his case, part of one glass of beer. And she wanted to get together with him, get something going. When he refused, Fran told Len they'd slept together anyway. Am I right so far?"

"Yes." Her mother's voice was small as she stared at the hotel carpeting.

"Then, Len wanted blackmail money. This is the part I can't understand. Dad…paid him. How could he do that? Why would he do that?"

"He just wanted to get rid of the man. Your dad thought that if he paid him off, Len wouldn't go to the police. Len kept saying he would if he didn't get any money from us. From Bob. I…kind of told him to."

"But that's so damning. Did Jackson Rogers find out about that?"

Her mother nodded.

"How?"

"Detective Rogers came here to question me. He waved the blackmail note in front of my face. I was scared of him. I said, 'But we paid him.' And then they went away for about an hour, then came back and handcuffed Bob."

Her mother had incriminated her father. How could she?

"So he took your word for it. Do you think they checked with Len?"

"Maybe."

"But, would Len tell the police about that? Wouldn't he deny it? What is he blackmailing Dad about, anyway? It couldn't be for having a drink."

Her mother didn't answer. Instead, she locked herself in the bathroom.

Tally was going to ask Detective Rogers if Len should be arrested for blackmail. Surely, that was a crime. Why was Len doing this? What was he holding over her parents' heads? The video of her dad handing money to Len? The long-ago partner switching? That didn't make sense. None of it felt right.

Tally was so befuddled!

When she started to drive home, she was so rattled she almost ran a red light. She stomped on her brakes to miss a car crossing the intersection on the green. The driver gave her a nasty look. She deserved it. After she got safely through the intersection, she pulled over to the curb to collect herself. There, before her, on a telephone pole, was a welcome diversion. One of Lily's posters caught her eye. Several people walking by stopped to notice it, too. Soon she felt calm enough to drive without causing an accident.

However, as she drove home slowly and carefully, she felt herself getting more depressed by the minute. All her woes clumped together, like poorly mixed batter, and refused to stay away from the surface of her thinking.

A shabby, derelict man stood at the side of the road, half on and half off the sidewalk, holding a cardboard sign, begging for help. As her car approached, he picked a duffel up off the ground, lowered his sign, and trudged away. She noticed that his hands and arms were covered with puckered burn scars. The sight brought Owen Herd's family into her mind. They had to live with the fact that he perished in the fire set by her parents' disgruntled employee. Did that haunt all of them every day? It should. She was angry with all of them. With Fran, Len, and with her parents, too.

* * * *

On Saturday night, when Yolanda saw that her sister was calling, she had a short pang of guilt. She should have called her. They hadn't talked for days. She walked from the kitchen to her brocade couch and sat to talk.

"Guess what, Yo?" Vi sounded happy. Yolanda was so glad to hear that. "Eden and I met her parents."

"I'm guessing it went better than meeting ours." She turned off the television. The news had just started and she didn't need to see that anyway.

"Oh, Yolanda. I'm so happy about this. Eden emailed them earlier in the week and said she wanted them to meet me."

"Did she say who you were? I mean, your relationship?"

"Totally. I helped her write it. She mentioned I'm Latina. She called me her girlfriend. Then she said we're serious about each other."

"That should do it." She traced the raised brocade pattern on the couch cushion. Should she say something about Kevin?

"Hey, listen to this. They had us to their country club today. We've been there for hours. We swam and had dinner."

"How nice! I'm so happy for you. They sound like lovely people."

"They are. They're just like Eden. Super-nice. And not at all upset about us being together, or me being part Hispanic."

"Did anyone talk about future plans?" Her couch cushions were so stiff. Maybe she should get a new couch. Something soft and more comfortable. Soft and comfortable didn't describe her relationship with Kevin right now. She kept hanging onto the fact that he was married.

"Not yet," Violetta said. "We didn't want to overwhelm them."

Yolanda wondered if her parents would have reacted better if this hadn't been sprung on them so suddenly.

Should she talk to her sister about that business with Kevin and his wife? She had to confide in someone.

Chapter 27

Tally dragged herself home after work on Saturday. She'd been crazy to think she could keep this up, being open seven days a week.

That was her first thought when she came in the door, kicked off her shoes, and collapsed onto her comfy couch.

Her second thought was that the reason she was worn out was because they had done so much business that day. Didn't that mean she *had* to stay open on Sundays? The shop was making too much money. She was trapped by her own success. She and Lily were the only ones working every day. Although Lily never seemed to flag, aside from that one bout of sickness. What would Tally do if she got sick, herself? That was a frightening prospect. Should she change her hours?

August was nearly over. She didn't want to change the scheduling setup now, during peak season. Maybe September would make a good breaking point to do something different. The tourists should slow down then, she hoped, until things picked up nearer to Christmas. She could try having Lily work five or six days and she could take one or two off herself, staggering their schedule.

She went over her employees in her mind, refusing to think about her dad, sitting in a jail cell waiting for more investigation, and her mother alone in the hotel. All three of the young women were finally shaping up to be better workers than when they started out. Lily was still the most reliable, but Molly and Greer had stopped taking smoking breaks, or vaping breaks, or whatever they called them. They were both showing up for work on time. Mostly.

Other thoughts, the ones she was trying not to think about, gave way to her worry about Greer's mother. That poor woman in that horrible nursing home. Tired as she was, Tally got up, changed into shorts and a T-shirt, and made herself go visit the woman. She refused to think about this trip serving as an excuse to not see her own parents.

Nigel protested with chirps when she headed for the door. He turned his back on her with his tail held high and stalked off into the bedroom.

The smell was even worse than she remembered. It hit her immediately when she went through the front door of the Setting Sun. She walked to the registration desk and asked if she could see Mrs. Tomson. The middle-aged woman behind the desk frowned.

"There's no one here by that name."

"I saw her Friday, day before yesterday. Has she left?"

"No one left this weekend. Our population is stable for now. In fact, we're full. No one is coming in or going out."

"I saw Mrs. Tomson. Her daughter was here and we both talked to her."

The woman shook her head. "No, no Mrs. Tomson."

"Could you double-check?"

She gave Tally an exasperated look. "I know all the residents. I don't have to check anything."

Was the woman not Greer's mother? Greer had told Tally so many lies, maybe this woman wasn't her mother after all. Tally tried once more. "Maybe she has a different name. Greer Tomson's mother."

The woman's brow cleared. "Oh, Greer's mother. Her name isn't Tomson. It's Samson."

There probably weren't two people with daughters named Greer. But there was something about that name. What was it? "Can I see her, please?" Tally kept to herself that she was probably going to make trouble for them, eventually, if the woman wasn't being cared for properly.

"She's in the TV room." She summoned a young woman standing nearby.

"Of course." With all the other zombies.

"I can show you the way." The young woman with apple-red cheeks, dressed as an aide, came forward and told Tally to follow her. "That's her, over there. I'll let you talk."

After the aide's smile to Greer's mother lit her pretty face, she left them alone and proceeded down the hallway.

Tally found a folding chair, pulled it over, and sat beside her. Greer's mother was in a wheelchair today. Tally attempted small talk, but Mrs. Samson only smiled and nodded at everything she said and didn't seem to understand her words. Were they overmedicating her? Tally wondered. She leaned in close to smell the woman, to see if she was in need of changing. Mrs. Samson smelled of baby powder, which relieved Tally. She did seem uncomfortable, though, squirming and shifting her weight. Just because she was powdered didn't mean she didn't have pressure wounds. Greer had mentioned that.

Tally studied her face. Maybe she was on a powerful painkiller, explaining her vacant expression. Tally did have to consider that the woman had no idea who she was. Maybe she would be more expressive if she knew Tally. To the older woman, Tally was probably just some strange person who sat next to her and started chatting.

On her way home, her mother phoned.

"They've let him go again."

Tally puffed out a breath of relief. "That's good."

"No, it's not. Wendell has been seen in the area."

"The one who burned your store, right?" Tally said.

"Yes, the man who escaped. The police told me he's been seen in the area."

"And they let Dad go because of that?"

"Yes, Wendell has a much better reason to want Fran dead. The detective also told me what killed her. Finally. Nicotine poisoning. Your dad had no access to that."

"Nicotine poisoning? What does that mean? Ground-up cigarettes?"

"No, he explained that there were massive amounts of it in her system. It probably came from those refills for the fake cigarettes. If Wendell Samson is around here, he could have had something to do with Fran's death."

Samson. Vaping. Tally's mouth hung open. Her mind patched the pieces together. She was hit by a flash of comprehension.

Samson was Greer's mother's name. Wendell Samson was her father. The pieces clicked. The puzzle came together like a perfected blended recipe.

She realized with a sudden clarity that she had seen Greer with her father, in the park, both of them vaping. That fit better than any explanation so far.

"The Whoopie Pies contained nicotine," her mother was saying. "Someone put it in them at our reception. Everyone knew all four of us would be there. Wendell must have gotten wind of our gathering somehow. We are all his enemies, according to him."

"I know how it was done," Tally said. "His daughter is working for me. Greer Tomson is really Greer Samson. Her driver's license has been altered, and I bet it was to change her last name. I even saw her in the park with him, using those vaping things. I'll bet she's the one who told Jackson that Dad was close to Fran all evening. I have to call Jackson right now."

She dialed his cell, but he didn't answer, so she called the station and left an urgent message for him to contact her, no matter what time it was.

Greer was scheduled to work tomorrow, Sunday. What should she do if Jackson didn't call her back tonight?

The rest of the drive home was a blur, her mind whirling with the disturbing thoughts running through her mind. She managed not to nearly run over anyone this time. Her mother, her own mother, had actually blurted out the blackmail details to the police. She could have predicted that would get him arrested again. Had Len admitted to the blackmail? She couldn't picture that.

Molly and Greer weren't the only ones who had problems with their mothers.

A painful thought shot through her mind like a bullet. Her mother and Len. Her parents had said that they had switched partners long ago. Who were these people? It was so hard to picture her parents doing that. They had all been in business together. It must have created an incestuous atmosphere.

Then the employee had burned the hardware store, killing another person, whom her parents had not taken care of like they'd promised.

Jackson returned Tally's call as she walked in the door of her house. Her living room smelled so pure and clean after the nursing home.

"Tally? What's so urgent?"

"I know what happened. It was Wendell Samson."

She heard his long-suffering sigh through the phone. "No, it was not Wendell Samson. He was nowhere near here when Fran was poisoned."

"Not him in person. His daughter. She did it for him."

"His daughter?"

"Greer, who works for me. She's his daughter. I just figured it out. Her mother is named Samson. In Setting Sun nursing home."

There was a moment of silence. "He does have a wife in a nursing home here. We've lost track of their daughter, though."

"She's going by a different name. She calls herself Greer Tomson. She gave me an altered driver's license for identification when I hired her. I saw her with Wendell in the park. They were both vaping. You need to arrest her tonight."

"Tally, I can't do that. I have to check things out. First, I have to see if she actually is his daughter."

"I can show you the copy of the falsified driver's license."

"Having a fake ID isn't enough to get you arrested for murder. Let me work on this. I promise I'll look into it."

Tally felt her heart hammering at the thought of working with Greer the next day. "Can you arrest her tonight, though?"

Another exasperated sigh. "No. I cannot arrest her tonight. I can't get anything done that fast. Relax. Let me look into it."

Tally paced, much to the consternation of Nigel, who meowed at her to sit down and furnish him a lap. She was too distraught to sit still. How could she work with Greer when she knew—yes, she knew—that Greer had poisoned Fran and tried to pin it on her own parents? And with no thought of who else might have died from the poisoned treats.

Could she fire Greer? Then she wouldn't have to work beside her. But that might anger the woman and endanger Tally's own life. Was Greer waiting to finish off the other three who hadn't been poisoned on her first try? How would she do it? When?

She went to bed, but was soon flopping over for the hundredth time, to Nigel's great distress. She threw off the covers and sat on the edge of her bed. Nigel thumped to the floor and brushed her legs.

She had been raised to be kind to others, to be thoughtful, considerate. Raised by her parents to be like that. But her parents weren't that way. At least they weren't back then. Maybe the past weighed on their minds? Was their punishing touring schedule a form of self-flagellation? Atonement? Everyone in town knew that Fran and Len had not had a good relationship. He'd gone after every dewy-eyed starlet who crossed the stage. Fran had become a hardened harridan, firing the ones her husband slept with and running roughshod over a lot of people's hopes and dreams. Were her parents more like Fran and Len and she just couldn't see it?

Rising, she went to her window and pulled the curtain back, staring at the streetlamp. The cat padded after her. She lifted him to feel his mighty purr. It comforted her.

Meanwhile, her parents had fled. They'd left Fredericksburg behind and lived a life of hotels and restaurants. They also left their children behind.

A lot of people had been hurt. Greer, most certainly, had killed Fran for her own father. Had probably tried to kill all four of them. Tally had believed, for a short time, that her own father had killed Fran. The thought haunted her as she gazed out her window, into the dark, nuzzled by a warm, furry, rumbling Nigel.

Chapter 28

In the morning, Tally felt like she wanted to throw up. The thought of working with Greer frightened her and made her feel queasy. She couldn't do it. She just couldn't work with her. Crossing her fingers and hoping Greer wouldn't think it suspicious, she decided to call her and tell her not to come in. Sunday would be busy, one of the busiest days of the week, but she would have Lily there to help.

"Hi Greer. This is Tally."

"I know," Greer said, maybe snapping a bit.

"You know, I don't think I need you to come in today."

"Why not?" Greer was definitely ticked off. "You know I need the money."

"It is short notice, isn't it? I'll pay you, okay?"

"What's going on? What are you doing?"

"Greer, I—I think I'll close early anyway. Something has come up. I need to concentrate on preparations for Monday."

"All the more reason I should be there."

"Well, no. It just won't work."

"Huh. How about Wednesday? Do you want me to work then?"

"Yes, I probably do." She would have to think of something else if Jackson didn't make a move by then. "Thanks very much for understanding."

"Uh, no, I don't understand at all."

"Thanks, Greer. I'll talk to you later."

Tally was breathing fast, sweating, and shaky. That had not gone well. Not well at all.

Nigel gave her a look that seemed sympathetic. She would assume it was. She needed sympathy right now, even if it was from a cat.

She was still shaky when she got to work. In fact, she had trouble getting her key into the keyhole of the back door. Lily pulled up in her small Honda as Tally finally got the door open and greeted her with a cheery, "Good morning, Tally. Isn't it a beautiful day?"

Tally looked up at the sky. It was a nice day. She hadn't been able to notice through her distress. Her mental state clouded the sky, colored the day gray, and dimmed the bright, late August sun.

Lily gave Tally a smile and swept past her to begin mixing, cooking, and baking treats for the day. Had Tally's life ever been that uncomplicated?

* * * *

Yolanda got a call from Kevin as soon as she arrived at work Sunday morning. After a few seconds of hesitation, she answered it.

"You're still speaking to me?" he asked.

The sound of his voice made her feel so good all over. What should she do? Go back with him? Take some time off? She worried that the kisses in the vineyard shed had been wrong. They had felt right, though.

"I need to talk to you about Monday," he said. "Are you about ready? Is there anything you need?"

"I'm pretty sure I am, unless I've forgotten something. I had the baskets done a week ago."

"When do you think I should start helping you bring over Tally's treats? And your baskets?"

Okay. He wasn't going to talk about it. She wouldn't, either. But she had to talk to someone. Tally. Soon.

"Kevin… I think we're both in good shape." He could take that any way he wanted to. In that second, the mists in her mind parted and she decided she wanted to stay with him. "We can bring our things over. I know—I'll close early today if you need help."

"How early?"

"Noon, okay? We'll have all afternoon and tomorrow morning. Everything will be set up beautifully for the wine tasting. In fact, I'll call Tally and see if she can bring her things over this afternoon, too."

"Perfect. Love you, Yo. Gotta go. Customers."

Love you. Maybe they would make it.

Yolanda called Tally's number, but didn't get her. She should have texted, she knew, but decided to leave a voice mail. Tally usually listened to those fairly often.

"I need to talk to you about…something. I don't want to leave a message or a text. Call me back when you have a few minutes."

Tally called back within seconds.

"I'm going to shut down at noon today," Yolanda said, "to help Kevin set up. Do y'all want to join us? Or do you need to stay open? I can get your things this afternoon and bring them over. It's all of a few feet, after all. Not a huge distance."

"That would be fine."

Tally sounded distracted. "Are y'all okay?" Yolanda asked.

"Yes, everything's fine."

"No, it's not, girlfriend. Something's bothering you."

"You're right. I can't keep secrets from you. One of my employees is… well, I think she might… Look, I can't talk about it right now, though. Later, okay?"

"Sure. Give me a call when you can."

Yolanda set her pink phone down on her sales counter and paused, wondering what was bothering Tally. Probably something to do with her father being accused of murder. What a mess that was!

She sent a text to Tally saying she would call her at noon.

"Yolanda?" Greer, Tally's employee, was standing in front of her. She hadn't heard her come in.

"Can I help you, Greer? Do you need a basket?"

"Yeah, maybe. But I'm really hot. Could I get a glass of cold water?"

Yolanda went to her sink in the back and filled a paper cup. "It's not all that cold," she said, coming back to the front and handing the cup to her. "But it should help if you're overheated. Have you been walking a lot outside?"

Greer drank half of the water. "I'll be okay. Thanks a lot." She set the cup on the counter and left.

Chapter 29

Tally should have known she couldn't fool Yolanda. Lily noticed her distress, too, Tally realized. She couldn't get Greer off her mind. The suspicion—no, she knew it was the fact—that Greer was a murderer was cutting a deep groove in her brain and everything else was falling into that abyss. She ruined a batch of fudge and turned it into a gooey mess, made the wrong change for customers three times in a row, and felt like she wanted to sit on the floor and cry.

"Tally, do you want to take a break?" Lily asked after Tally handed a customer Twinkies when they had asked for Mary Janes.

"Maybe I should."

"Are you getting sick?"

Tally seized on that for an explanation. She didn't want to discuss her suspicions, her knowledge, of Greer with Lily. If she was right, that would endanger Lily. "I might be. I don't feel very well."

"Do you want to go home? I can call Greer to come in. She's supposed to be here today anyway."

Tally did not want to have Greer in, if she could avoid that. "No! I mean, no, that won't be necessary. Molly's here. I'm sure I'm not contagious. It's something I ate. I'll take a break in the kitchen for a few minutes, if you don't mind."

"Go ahead and take a short rest, at least. Take your time. You have to be ready for tomorrow. Molly and I will handle things out here. I can holler if I get overrun."

Tally was so grateful for Lily. She must think of a way to show her deep appreciation for her as a dependable employee. And as a non-murderer.

* * * *

Yolanda waited on a young couple who wanted to celebrate their first anniversary with a basket. He had picked out some items for his new bride and she had bought some things for her young groom. They were so loving and sweet, a beautiful couple. Yolanda wanted to do an extra-special job for them. They didn't need the basket for two weeks, so she had plenty of time to do a suitable, maybe spectacular arrangement for them.

After they left, she sat down to sketch out some design ideas. She glanced around for her phone to look up what the first-anniversary theme was. The traditional one was paper, she remembered, but there was also a more modern one. Her phone wasn't on the counter where she usually laid it, so she started roaming the shop, looking for it. It was bright pink. She should be able to find it.

When was the last time she used it? To call and text Tally. It should be right here.

* * * *

Tally was in her office with the door closed, but not relaxing. Not taking it easy. She was distracted and fretting. She needed to tell Yolanda what was going on.

Like a sign from above, her phone dinged. She pulled it from her pocket to find a text from Yolanda. Eagerly, she clicked on it.

meet me at the vin yard

Stupid autocorrect. She knew Yolanda would never spell *vineyard* that way. She answered, puzzled.

What are you doing at the vineyard?

The answer came immediately.

important emergency come quick

What on earth was Yolanda doing way out at Kevin's vineyard? Right now, she should be either in her shop getting things ready for Monday, or in his, helping him do the same. Maybe she had gone there with him to pick up some extra wine.

Tell me. What is it?

There was no answer. She waited a good five minutes. Before this, she had felt mildly queasy. Now she felt a lot more so. Something was very wrong.

She went to the front, where Lily and Molly were both surrounded by customers. Taking Lily aside as she apologized to the buyers, she whispered to her, "Something is very wrong. Yolanda sent me a strange text. It doesn't even sound like her. I think I have to go check it out."

"Go, go," Lily urged. "We'll be fine."

"Are you sure? I hate to leave you right now. But something is wrong. I have a very bad feeling about those texts."

"Come on. You've been useless today anyway. Go see what's wrong with Yolanda. We'll be fine. Don't worry."

"Lily, you're the best." She wanted to kiss her. Grabbing her purse on her way to the back door, she jumped into her Chevy Sonic and took off.

Chapter 30

Tally pulled onto the dirt and gravel road to Kevin's place, Bear Mountain Vineyards, about five miles southeast of town. His grapevines and fermenting building were located here, since his tasting room was in town. The sole building on this end of the property was a small storage shed for equipment. She bumped along the rough road, wondering where exactly Yolanda was. There was a truck parked next to the shed, but it wasn't Yolanda's sporty Nissan Rogue. It was a dirty green pickup that looked unfamiliar. At first. She took a second look. Had she seen it somewhere before?

She parked beside it and drew out her phone to text.

I'm here. Where are you?

She waited a minute or so before she got another message.

get out of your car walk straight from the back of the shed

Why? What's going on, Yo?

There was no answer.

She opened her car door and got out, listening. She heard nothing but droning insects and a breeze stirring the leaves of the acres of grape plants. The heat pressed down onto her head and shoulders, trying to grind her into the soil.

"Yo!" she called out. "Yolanda!"

No reply.

Not all of her sweat was from the heat. Ripples of apprehension ran up her arms and her spine. She took a few steps toward the shed, then stopped. She sent a quick text to Jackson, telling him where she was and that something was very wrong with Yolanda. Then she looked at the truck again. It wasn't Yolanda's. Had she seen it somewhere before, though?

Maybe. If so, where? Maybe Yolanda wasn't even here. Someone else was, though. Did they have Yo's phone? They must have, she thought.

Here suspicion was confirmed with the next text she received.

we have yolana. follow instructons and she wont get hurt NOW

She sent another quick text to Jackson.

Don't call or text Yolanda. Come to the vineyard ASAP.

Then she headed out, walking between the rows of eight-foot-tall trellises, her palms prickling and the hairs on the back of her neck standing as upright as the grape plants.

* * * *

Yolanda remembered what she had been doing when she set her phone on the countertop. Greer had been in the shop, acting strangely, asking for water, then only drinking a bit of it. Had she taken her phone? She picked up her landline to call Tally's shop and got Lily.

"Tally's not here," Lily said. "I thought she went to talk to you. She said she was worried about some texts from you."

She was also worried about an employee. Greer. She knew it. And her phone was missing right after Greer was in her shop. "Oh, no," Yolanda wailed. "*No no no.* Did she say where she was going?"

"Well, no. I thought she went to your shop."

"How long ago?"

"Gosh, it was over half an hour, I think."

Yolanda ended the call and perched on her stool, thinking so hard her head hurt. Greer had her phone and had texted Tally. And had gotten Tally to go...somewhere. Where? She called the police station and learned that Detective Jackson Rogers had headed out five minutes ago.

"Where did he go?" she asked.

"Let me see. He told me and I wrote it down," the dispatcher-receptionist said.

There was a long, maddening pause. Yolanda wanted to scream, *Hurry up! Something is very wrong!*

"Here it is. He went to the vineyard. That's what he said. I don't know what that means. There are a lot of vineyards around here."

"Thanks, I think I know."

Had Greer told Tally to drive to Kevin's vineyard? Why would she do that? And why was the detective on his way there? Did Tally call him? Did someone else? Had something terrible happened?

Chapter 31

Tally parted her lips slightly to quiet her breathing so she wouldn't be heard by whoever was hiding out here in the vineyard.

She slowly tiptoed through the tall rows of trellises, as quietly as she could, but didn't hear anything. A rustle in the leaves made her jerk her head around, but no one was there.

Squinting ahead, she thought she saw a shadow moving behind the plants to her right. Then to her left. They were here. Somewhere. Where?

The vision of the green pickup flashed through her mind. It had picked Greer up from work, long before any of them knew that Wendell Samson had escaped from prison.

Without warning, Greer and a man Tally instantly knew was her father sprung upon her, pinning her to the ground. The man held her body down with strong arms and a knee to her chest. Greer clamped a hand over Tally's mouth, stifling her attempted scream. Greer shucked a backpack off her shoulders, letting it drop in the soft soil.

The look of glee on Greer's face horrified Tally. Greer glanced to her father for approval and he nodded, stretching her smile even wider.

"Good job, darlin'."

"Thanks, Dad. Now we need to get rid of her."

"I guess we do, if she's figured everything out like you said. You know what to do next."

Greer produced a vial of liquid from a backpack on the ground one-handed and lifted it to Tally's lips. "Drink this," she snarled.

Tally knew what it was. It was the vaping liquid that had killed Fran Abraham. She wasn't about to swallow it. She clamped her lips tight and shook her head from side to side.

"Hold still," Wendell growled. "You're gonna swallow this."

Greer forced the vial between Tally's lips and tipped a few drops of it into her mouth, but Tally spit it up into Greer's face.

"Now you've made me mad." Greer sat back on her heels, her face red from the exertion and the heat.

"Go ahead, tie her up," Wendell said. "We'll do something else."

Greer pulled a length of rope from her backpack with her free hand, handed it to her father, then fished out a rag. She roughly wound the rag around Tally's head, shoving it into her mouth and gagging her. The cloth smelled like a dirty garage floor. At least it wouldn't kill her, like the liquid nicotine would.

Wendell took the rope from Greer and trussed Tally's hands behind her, pulling on the rope to tie the knots. He jerked her arms and sat her up, then wound the rope around the stakes holding up some of the vines, threading it through the plant and the trellis. She ended up sitting with her back to the grape vine, securely fastened and gagged. What else were they planning for her?

Her heart hammered and her breath, behind the filthy cloth, was shallow and fast. Her vision grayed around the edges. She would not pass out. She willed herself to fight the panic. Slowing her breathing, she closed her eyes and felt the fear recede.

She imagined Jackson getting her message, heading out here, and not being able to find her. The tall plants hid everything unless you were lined up with the exact row they were in. She pulled at her bonds and tried to shake the plant to make some noise, but it didn't budge.

"What do I do with this phone?" Greer asked, holding up Yolanda's pink phone. How had Greer stolen Yolanda's phone? Had they harmed Yolanda?

"Yeah, we'll have to get rid of that. Let me think." Wendell scratched the three-day growth on his face with a papery sound. His scruffy beard was streaked with gray and didn't add anything to his harsh looks. His forehead and cheeks were furrowed, like something had raked his face and left rows big enough to plant seeds in.

"Should we just bury it here, with her?" Greer asked.

They were facing away from her, conferring with their heads together, but not caring if she overheard them. Tally flinched.

Her legs and bottom were suddenly ablaze with pain. She looked down.

She was sitting on a pile of fire ants.

She had to move.

"No, we can't do that," Wendell said. "They'll find her body eventually and we don't want 'em to find the phone, too."

"You're right. All those texts are on it. Someone might figure out what we did."

Pulling at the stake she was tied to, she felt it move slightly. The ground, which was plowed every spring and fall, was soft. If she could pull the stake out of the earth, she could get away.

"Hey, Dad, we should take her phone, too. It has all the texts we sent. They're in both phones."

"You're right."

Tally gave a mighty jerk. The wood came out of the ground, but was still entangled in the woody plant.

They hadn't noticed her movements, still conferring together and not paying any attention to their securely-bound captive.

Carefully, ignoring the ant bites, working through the pain, she slipped the rope off the bottom of the stake.

"It's probably in her purse, Dad."

Tally's purse was a few feet away, in the next row, where she'd dropped it when they captured her. They stepped through the opening they'd created to ambush her, into the next row.

Tally sprang to her feet and ran.

Chapter 32

The party was in full swing at Bear Mountain Vineyards. Tally strolled through the large room, up and down the rows of wine racks, chatting with the happy customers who were drinking wine and sampling her wares. She was so grateful that no one was afraid to taste her sweet products. They even ate the Whoopie Pies. Yolanda took orders for gift baskets containing wares from both Tally and Kevin's places at a table near the front.

The calamine didn't take away all the pain from the fire ant bites, but she refrained from scratching the backs of her legs or, even worse, her bottom. How would that look?

Lily paused on her way past, holding out a tray of stemmed goblets. "Great turnout."

Tally took a glass of wine. Her second. "Yes, I guess our publicity worked. Excuse me, I should say *your* publicity worked."

"Dorella is doing a great job," Lily said, watching the young woman's curly blond head going back and forth behind the bar, helping Kevin serve drinks from there. "I'm glad you asked her to work tonight."

Tally looked at Dorella, too, pleased that she had agreed to Tally's proposal. "She's going to start at the shop in a couple of days."

"Great! I really like her."

Cole had left, but had promised Dorella to return soon to see her. Dorella also, she told Tally, was going to visit him on the road. It was possible that they would stay together, difficult as that might be with Cole's traveling job.

Lily lowered her voice to ask Tally, "How did you get out of the police station so soon?"

"Detective Rogers knew this was going on, so he let me go after a brief interview. I have to go back tomorrow to give my official statement and sign it."

"Okay. Molly and I can run the shop."

Tally spotted Mrs. Gerg hesitating at the front door. She hurried up to her and offered her a glass of wine. Mrs. Gerg took it and downed the whole thing in three noisy gulps. "I'm so glad I found you."

"Is everything all right?"

"Oh, yes, perfectly. Perfectly all right. I had to find you right away after I found this." She extracted a complicated mass of metal from her purse. After she shook it out, Tally could see it was, of course, a necklace, one with a great number of adornments handing from the main chain.

"See?" Mrs. Gerg said, proudly. "It's candy. Like your shop."

Tally took it and examined the large pendants. Some were lollipops, oblong candy bars, and some were in the shape of wrapped candies with twists of paper at both ends. The lollipop sticks and the edges of the metal paper twists looked dangerous.

"It's lovely," Tally said. "Perfect. Thank you so much." Cautiously, she put it over her head and draped it around her neck. Luckily, she wasn't wearing a low-cut top. She hoped the metal wouldn't rip her clothing.

The chirp of her cell phone cut through the murmurs of the crowd and Tally stepped to the side of the room to answer it, though she didn't recognize the number.

"Sweetheart!" It was her mother!

"How's it going?" Tally asked. "You got there okay?"

"Yes, we made it to Singapore in record time. No delays, no lost luggage."

"You deserve some good fortune after what we've all just gone through." Tally heard her dad's voice in the background, but couldn't understand his words.

"Yes, dear, I'll tell her," Tally's mother said to him. "He wants you to know how well our show went. We hardly had time to rehearse at all and we're working with a bunch of musicians we've never worked with before."

"Y'all are pros, Mom. That shouldn't be a problem."

"In fact, it's one of the best shows we've ever put on. Here's your dad."

Her dad's voice came on. "Your mom is right. Hardly any rehearsal, no sleep, and we pulled it off. We have another show tomorrow, then we're going to take a day off before our next gig."

A day off. Tally smiled. If it were her, she'd probably need a week off. The stamina of her parents amazed her.

"Hey, break a leg. Keep breaking your legs. You're doing great."

They said their good-byes. Tally wondered when she would next see her parents.

She felt someone touch her arm and turned.

"I had to come to see this," a young woman said.

Her pretty, round face and rosy cheeks looked familiar, but Tally couldn't place her.

"I'm an aide at Setting Sun. I met you when you visited Mrs. Samson."

"Oh, yes, now I remember you. You helped me find her in the TV room."

"This is very fun."

Tally snagged a glass of wine from the tray as Lily passed by again and handed it to her. "It's nice of you to come."

"I do hope you visit Mrs. Samson again. She gets lonely."

Tally felt a pang, knowing that she would be even lonelier in the future, with her daughter locked up in prison. "I'd like to do that." Tally had a sudden inspiration. "In fact, I'd like to organize some people to regularly visit the ones whose families don't come often."

"Some of them don't have anyone visit. Ever."

"How sad."

"That would be a wonderful thing." The young nursing aide's cheeks glowed as she sipped the wine and gave Tally a broad grin. "I'm so glad I talked to you."

"I'm glad, too."

Tally made a mental note to get that project going as soon as she could. That way, something good would result from the trouble with Greer and her father. She felt her heart glowing to match the young aide's pretty face.

Note from the author:

Some actual businesses and institutions of Fredericksburg were used. Others were invented. I tried to faithfully represent the existing places that were used, but changed the library hours to suit the story.

Recipe

Whoopie Pies

Cookie tops and bottoms
Make these first:

1/2 cup butter, softened
1 cup white sugar

1 egg
1 cup evaporated milk
1 teaspoon vanilla extract

2 cups all-purpose flour
1/2 teaspoon salt
1/2 cup unsweetened cocoa powder
1 1/2 teaspoons baking soda
1/2 teaspoon baking powder

Cream the butter and sugar together in a large mixing bowl. Add the next three ingredients, mixing well.

In a separate bowl, combine the dry ingredients. Then slowly add this to the large bowl, while mixing, until combined. Don't overmix.

Drop the dough onto a greased cookie sheet by the tablespoonful, leaving 3 inches between them.

Bake at 400 degrees for 6–8 minutes. Press with a finger and they should be firm. Cool at least one hour. Then fill.

Marshmallow filling
Make this while the cookie tops and bottoms are cooling.

1/2 cup butter, softened
1 cup confectioners' sugar
1/2 teaspoon vanilla extract

1 cup marshmallow crème

Blend all until smooth. Spread 1 to 2 tablespoons of filling on the flat side of a cookie piece and cover with another cookie piece.

Enjoy!

adapted from Allrecipes.com by Jody Crout

If you enjoyed DEADLY SWEET TOOTH,
by
Kaye George

Be sure not to miss the next book in the
Vintage Sweets Mysteries

Turn the page for a quick peek at
INTO THE SWEET HEREAFTER
Enjoy!

Chapter 1

Tally Holt opened her eyes to the startlingly close orbs of her big black and white Maine Coon cat, Nigel. He stared earnestly, communicating his desire for breakfast with his sheer willpower. She smiled and rubbed the top of his head to start his purring motor. She loved the volume he put out.

"Move, silly, so I can get the sheet off me." She shoved him gently so she could peel back the sheet and sit up. It was too warm to use covers, really, but she always felt better when she was covered with something.

Nigel padded after her into the kitchen of her small Fredericksburg house. Sun poured in through the windows, filtered by the old live oaks in the front yard. Later, when the relentless Texas sun rose higher, the trees would shade the whole house. After she scooped the cat food into his dish and refilled his water bowl, she cleaned the litter.

Cats are so easy, she thought. *That took less than five minutes and he's set until tonight.*

She hadn't grown up with any pets, but knew, from observation, that dogs required a lot more maintenance. It had been a long time since she got mad at her brother, Cole, for dumping Nigel on her. He had broken up with one of his many girlfriends and she didn't take Nigel with her.

She had to admit, she liked to come home to a warm, living being at night after she closed up her shop. But before that, she would need to get dressed and actually open it.

Soon she was blowing an ignored kiss to Nigel and heading out the front door.

* * * *

Tally and her best friend Yolanda Bella beamed, delighted with the window display Yolanda had just finished putting together. Lily Vale, Tally's young employee, and Raul Fuentes, Yolanda's trusted assistant in the basket shop were behind them, grinning. They stood on the warm sidewalk outside Bella's Baskets in Fredericksburg, Texas, where tourist season was moving into high gear.

Tally turned to her favorite employee. "Lily, the plastic candies look exactly like the real thing. They're wonderful."

The plastic replicas of the vintage sweets that Tally sold next door at Tally's Olde Tyme Sweets nestled in various gift baskets, some handmade locally, some bought and reconditioned by Yolanda herself. Lily had come up with the idea to use the replicas last year. The ones they'd been using had gotten faded and old looking, so Lily looked for another place to buy the replicas. She had searched sources and decided on this one. The fake candies were made in Southeast Asia from custom molds modeled after sketches Lily had sent them. They were not only much cheaper, but were environmentally friendly, according to the ads.

"I'm glad they got here so soon," Lily said. "This is kind of a celebration of your one-year mark."

Tally hadn't thought of that. It was a year ago, mid-June, when she had opened her shop with high hopes, which had mostly panned out. Her shop and Yolanda's were both thriving after some early struggles. She swelled with pride, looking over the colorful display that married her vintage candy products and Yolanda's gift baskets.

The colorful baskets held items to go with the themes people usually wanted: birthdays (candles, party hats, small gifts wrapped in birthday paper), anniversaries (photo albums, silk roses, tin stars in a ten-year basket and silver stars in a twenty-five year one), and new house celebrations (small houses from a toy store, bags of grass seed for the new lawns, Monopoly dollar bills).

Strewn among the baskets were boughs from dogwood trees with silk blossoms, and a few silk crepe myrtles, since it was spring in Texas Hill Country.

People strolled past, perusing the displays of the touristy shops of Fredericksburg and enjoying a soft, warm day before summer descended upon the town in earnest. Of course, in Texas, a merely warm day meant it was in the high eighties rather than the nineties. Not that full summer heat would deter the tourists and local shoppers. The small German-founded town was a popular shopping, dining, and wine-tasting destination for much of the year.

Tally's landlady, Mrs. Gerg, shuffled up to the group.

"My, doesn't that look nice." Mrs. Gerg stuck her head forward to peer at the display. "Aren't you afraid the chocolate will melt on those Moon Pies? They look like real ones, not those plastic ones you were using." She gave Tally a worried look. "It's warm, and the sun is hitting the window this morning." It was shining full onto the baskets, the better for everyone to see them.

Tally smiled and waved a hand toward Lily. "We can thank Lily for those. This has been all her idea and she found a very reasonable place to get new ones. They're all biodegradable plastic."

"Compostable, really," Lily added.

Mrs. Gerg took another look at the goodies, glistening through the glass. "So they are. Very good, Lily. How clever of you."

Lily beamed. Tally noticed the way Raul was looking at the young woman. His eyes looked a bit…lovestruck. Was this new? She had never noticed the attraction between the two of them before. Lily returned a similar moon-struck gaze to the dark, handsome young man.

Some of the passersby paused to admire the wares also, creating a bit of a blockage in the flow of foot traffic. One man, hobbling past on a pair of crutches, stopped, too, staring at the window intently. Tally followed his gaze and took a harder look at the replicas. Some of them looked lopsided. Were they melting? The spring sun that shone on Fredericksburg could be as hot as a summer sun in a lot of other places. They were only slightly misshapen. Should they take them out of the window? Maybe they would last through the week, then they would decide what to do. Put them somewhere else? Get a refund for faulty replicas?

The man on crutches noticed Tally paying attention to him and quickly turned to stump a few steps away.

Yolanda sneezed three times in a row, whipping a tissue out of her pocket. Tally knew she kept them ever-present in the spring for her allergies.

"How's the crime watch going, Mrs. Gerg?" Yolanda asked, tucking her tissue pack into her pocket. Mrs. Gerg was a member of the newly founded neighborhood group calling themselves Crime Fritzers, after a popular nickname for Fredericksburg, Fritztown.

"It's getting off the ground." Mrs. Gerg grinned at all four of them. "We're determined to keep crime down in our beautiful city."

Tally didn't think the crime rate was very high, but fighting it gave Mrs. Gerg something constructive to do and kept her from a hobby of hers—collecting things to give to Tally from garage and yard sales around town. Tally was running out of room to store the cheap treasures Mrs. Gerg delighted in bringing her. She hadn't received any in three weeks, since the Crime Fritzers started their organized patrols, so Tally was in favor of the group.

Mrs. Gerg walked away in her ancient shoes with rundown heels. She had walked miles in them during the time Tally knew her, so Tally had quit worrying about her feet.

Lily lurched forward, shoved from behind by a careless pedestrian. The offender hurried off without saying "excuse me" and Tally caught Lily so she wouldn't fall into the glass window.

"Are you all right?"

Lily straightened up. "I'm fine." She winced.

"Is your back hurt?" Tally held her arm lightly, to make sure she stayed upright.

"I think I took an elbow, but it'll be okay."

"You're sure? I can get you some ice."

Lily waved Tally off. "No, no, I'm fine. Really."

"I think that guy hit you with his crutch," said Raul, touching Lily's back, where she'd been pushed. Lily turned to face Raul and gave him a radiant smile.

Tally saw the concern on Raul's face as they gazed at each other. Yes, there was something there, something sizzling between them.

* * * *

Yolanda and Raul went back inside Bella's Baskets and Tally and Lily returned to Tally's Olde Tyme Sweets to finish up their work day. Molly Kelly was holding down the fort, that is, the sweet shop, waiting on a group of Red Hat ladies who wanted treats for their next meeting. The local Red Hat Society had a large chapter and Tally was glad when they'd decided to use her as their official meeting treat supplier a few months back.

Tally retired to the kitchen, behind the sales room, to whip up a batch of Mallomars since the glass display case was low on them. In the sales room, Lily tied on her pink smock, designed to match the muted, swirling pinks and lilacs on the walls, and greeted the next group to come through the front door and sound the soft chime, three teenaged boys who looked hungry.

At a few minutes past seven, Tally closed up and walked the few blocks to the house she rented from Mrs. Gerg, on East Schubert Street. Nigel greeted her at the door. If he were a dog, his tail would be wagging. As it was, he started talking to her in his cheerful chirps, no doubt inquiring about din-din time.

"Soon," Tally reassured him. "I just need to get my slippers on and pour a glass of iced tea. Then you'll get yours."

Now, in mid-June, the temperature was still in the high sixties this time of night. She'd gotten warm walking home. After they had both eaten, she took him into the back yard in his harness.

"Look, Nige." She pointed through the small leaves of the live oak. "Full moon tonight. Isn't it beautiful?"

For just a moment, she felt sorry for herself, sitting outside, under a romantic full moon, the smell of jasmine wafting on the slight breeze, with a cat as her only companion. But the thought of Raul and Lily and the looks they'd given each other brought a smile to her lips. The perfect evening seemed to call for thoughts of romance, even if it weren't her romance.

* * * *

The next morning, Yolanda arrived at her shop, Bella's Baskets, in a good mood. In the last few years, she'd had differences with her overbearing father, who didn't think she had what it took to make her business succeed. But last night she'd taken a check over to the ranch her parents owned on the outskirts of town.

When he opened the front door, she stuck the check out. "This will repay one fourth of what I've borrowed from you," she said.

She got a kick out of his blank stare. He took the check and looked at the amount, then frowned. "Can you afford this?"

She twisted a strand of her hair, trying to act nonchalant. This was a big moment for her, but she didn't want him to know that. "I said I'd repay you, and I am."

"I don't want you to run out of cash," he said.

That was her problem. He always thought she needed rescuing, needed taken care of. What she needed was to be treated as an adult.

"I'll let you know when I have the next payment." She had driven away, pleased with herself. She hadn't taken any of his bait, had remained calm. And the truth was, she *could* afford the amount she had given him. Business was very good.

In the morning, if she'd known how to whistle, she would have been whistling as she came through the back door, greeted by the heady smell of lilies. The whiff she took tickled her nose and brought out a couple of big sneezes.

Her employee must have laid the bunch of lilies on the counter earlier. He was now at the front of the shop.

"Miss Yolanda!" Raul looked stricken. "Look what happened."

Bright sunlight streamed through her display window. Then she noticed the rays glinting off the shards. The window was broken.

* * * *

Heading down the sidewalk to open her store, Tally Holt saw a commotion ahead.

"Tally, look!" Yolanda shouted and waved her forward. She sounded distraught.

When Tally approached, she could see why. The sidewalk before Bella's Baskets sparkled with broken glass. The window had been smashed.

"What happened?" Tally asked. There hadn't been a storm. Someone must have broken it, but why?

"Somebody threw a rock through my window," Yolanda wailed.

Tally took a good look, well, as good as she could, through the police personnel photographing and measuring.

"They're gone!" Yolanda pointed at the window.

Tally looked more closely. The new plastic replicas were gone.

Who would steal cheap plastic pieces of candy?

And why did the window smell so lovely? Tally peered inside the store and saw Raul arranging some stargazer lilies on the work counter. That's what she smelled, the lilies.

Detective Jackson Rogers emerged from the knot of police personnel. "Tally, you and Yolanda come over here. I need to let you know what happened."

They joined him a few feet away from the growing crowd. "It looks like someone stole the plastic candies," Tally said. "Is that right?"

"Yes, to begin with." Detective Rogers glanced at the notepad he was holding. "At four a.m. a member of the local crime watchers group observed a brick being thrown through the window and one party scooping up the plastic pieces."

"Oh, so you caught the thief?"

"Tally, stop interrupting me." Jackson's words were stern, but he smiled when he said them. He grew serious as he continued. "The crime watcher was beaten and the thief escaped with the goods. We got a description and think we should be able to apprehend him soon."

"Someone got beat up?" Yolanda put a hand to her mouth. "Was it bad?"

"He's in the hospital." The detective looked at his notes. "A member of the neighborhood watch group."

"A 'he' and not a 'she?' For sure?" Tally asked. "Not Mrs. Gerg? She's a member of that group. They go on patrol in the downtown at night."

Detective Jackson gave his head a slight shake. "We've asked them to stay in their vehicles. They're not supposed to apprehend anyone. Unfortunately, this is what can happen. But no, not Mrs. Gerg. It's a member of her group, though. It's the…" he consulted his notes again "…Crime Fritzers. They're not supposed to be alone. They are always supposed to patrol in pairs."

"Yes, that's her group. And the injured man was in the group? In the Crime Fritzers?"

The detective smiled. "Crime Fritzers. Yeah." He chuckled. "Sorry. Funny name."

Tally had to smile too.

"But you don't have the thieves," Yolanda said. "Does anyone have any idea why they were stealing those? They're not expensive."

"They're a little too cheap, in fact," Tally said. "Lily ordered them because they were economical and environmentally friendly. But it turns out that means they dissolve."

"Really?" Yolanda turned to her. "You didn't tell me that."

"Did you notice they were starting to melt yesterday in the sun?" Tally said. "I asked Lily about them last night before we closed and she told me. She noticed they were melting, too, but didn't want to say anything. She hoped they would hold up. I thought they would, too. I was going to leave them a few more days."

Yolanda threw her head back. Tally thought she might be asking for strength from above.

"I know, Yo. We should have just taken them out."

"Are you finished?" Jackson asked. "I need to get back to work."

"Wait," Tally said. "Is there any reason he wanted to steal them?"

"We're working on that," he said, and walked off, leaving Tally and Yolanda looking at each other, perplexed.

"I wonder when we can clean up this mess," Yolanda said.

The crime scene tape came down at about noon and Yolanda called Tally, whose shop had opened nearly on time and was doing a booming business. Probably, she thought, because the crime team with their bright yellow tape was a draw for curiosity seekers. Once they had checked out the basket shop activity, they naturally walked next door and were lured into the sweet shop.

"Can you spare a minute, or one of your workers, to help me get my window cleaned up?" Yolanda asked Tally when she answered her cell phone. "I have someone coming later today to put in a new window."

"You got same-day service. Great. I can come myself. I think everyone in town has been here today already, so it's slowing down now."

Tally called to her employees that she was going out to help Yolanda. Three young women currently worked for her. Molly Kelly and Lily Vale worked every day but Monday, the day the shop was closed. Her third employee, Dorella Diggs, came in Wednesday and Friday. On those days, Tally could afford to take time away from the shop.

"I might as well do some shopping for the store if there's time after I help Yolanda."

"Will you be back by closing?" Lily asked from behind the counter, where she was ringing up a sale on a bag of Mallomars.

"I'm not sure. It's a mess, with all the broken glass. Can you just close up if I'm not back by seven?"

"Sure. Don't worry about it."

Tally wouldn't. She, finally, had three dependable, trustworthy women working for her. It made her life easy.

As she walked up to the window where Yolanda was leaning into the opening, carefully picking glass shards off the floor of the display space, a white pickup parked at the curb. A magnetic sign on the side of it advertised "Ozzy's Odd Jobs" with a local phone number in bright red lettering.

A small man jumped out. "Which one is Mizz Bella?" He looked at Tally first and she pointed to Yolanda.

Yolanda straightened up. "You brought the window already? Great."

He unclipped a large piece of glass from the holder on the side of his truck.

Tally whispered to Yolanda, "Are you sure it's the right size? How did he know how big a piece of glass to bring?"

Yolanda laughed. "He came and measured it before."

Tally nodded, reassured.

"Wait just a sec," Yolanda said. "We need to get the rest of this debris out of here." She dashed inside and came back with a large paper bag. She and Tally scooped up what was left of the broken glass, taking care not to cut their fingers. Tally spotted some other debris, some things that weren't broken glass. She leaned farther into the window and decided it was pieces of a broken plastic Moon Pie. As she picked them up, shiny green stones fell out. She gathered those, too, and stuck everything into the bag. They would be able to easily remove the baskets and other décor from inside, but this clean up of the floor was much easier from the front.

"Okay, we're done." Yolanda gestured toward the open space with the shards of remaining broken window glass.

He moved with precision and speed and had the broken pieces removed and the window replaced in what seemed like minutes as Tally and Yolanda watched.

After, he said he'd send a bill, the two women stood looking at what was left of the display for a moment. The baskets remained, full of goodies and beribboned to match their themes. The dogwood and crepe myrtle boughs were still there, too, and undamaged.

"I guess I have to redo the whole window now," Yolanda said.

"It doesn't look that bad. It's just that the candies are missing. If you didn't know they'd been there, you wouldn't think anything is wrong. We have a few more, but they would just look lonely if we put them in there."

"You're right. I'm exhausted. You want to get a snack?"

"Yes, I can do that. I didn't know how long this would take so I told the girls I might not be back. But your shop is still open. Can you leave?"

"Ha. You notice I haven't had any customers since you came. I'll tell Raul to close up. Let's go celebrate surviving the Broken Window Incident."

Tally grinned. "Let's."

About the Author

Taken by Megan Russow

One of Kaye George's quirky claims to fame is having lived in nine states, many of which begin with the letter 'M.' Though a native Californian, Kaye moved to Moline, Illinois, at the tender age of 3 months. After college at Northwestern University in Evanston, IL, and marriage to Cliff during finals week their senior year, she and Cliff touched upon Sumter, SC, Lompoc, CA (very briefly), and Great Falls, Montana, during his Air Force career.

Kaye is also a violinist, an online mystery reviewer, an award winning short story writer, and the author of four different mystery series with three different publishers and one self published. She has accrued four Agatha Award nominations and one finalist position for the Silver Falchion, as well as national bestseller status with her Fat Cat series written as Janet Cantrell.

Kaye George

Revenge is Sweet

The Vintage
Sweets
Mysteries

UNDERGROUND

LYRICAL